GOODBYE MR. SPALDING

GOODBYE MR. SPALDING

STORIES BY
BRUCE MEYER

Black Moss Press

© Copyright Bruce Meyer 1995

This book is published by Black Moss Press at 2450 Byng Road, Windsor, Ontario N8W 3E8. It is published with the grateful assistance of the Canada Council, the Ontario Arts Council and the Department of Canadian Heritage.

Black Moss books are distributed in Canada and the U.S. by Firefly Books. Orders in Canada should be directed to Firefly, 250 Sparks Avenue, Willowdale, Ontario M2H 2S4.
In the U.S., orders should be sent to P.O. Box 1338 Ellicott Station, Buffalo, New York 14205.

Canadian Cataloguing in Publication Data:

Meyer, Bruce, 1957-
   Goodbye Mr. Spalding: stories

ISBN 0-88753-282-9

   I. Title.
PS8576.E93G6 1995   C813'.54   C95-900504 8
Pr9199.3.M49G6 1995

This book is for Kerry.

Acknowledgements

"Horse Diving" and "Long Way Up, Short Way Down" appeared previously in *Dugout*.

"The Death of Grass" appeared previously in *Radio Silence* by Bruce Meyer (Windsor, Ontario: Black Moss Press, 1992).

Cover art and frontice piece by Arthur Burdett Frost (1907) hand tinted and supplied courtesy of Guenther Dreeke, The Dickinson Gallery, Toronto.

I am grateful to Thomas Heitz and Robert Browning of the National Baseball Hall of Fame and Museum Incorporated of Cooperstown, New York for their assistance with research materials and information on Cannonball Crane, Al Travers, the Sunset League, and the Spalding World Tour of 1888.

Thanks also to the Cooperstown Hall of Fame for the honourary Lifetime Pass.

I also wish to thank those who assisted me with this book: Bill Humber of Seneca College for his support and information on Albert Spalding; Russell Field of *Dugout* for his encouragement, support and for information on early baseball in Toronto; Black Moss Press and Exile Editions/ *Exile* for support through the Writers' Reserve Fund of the Ontario Arts Council; Fred Howe for information on Babe Ruth's first home run; Mark Levin for information on Ty Cobb; Barry Callaghan for his encouragement and advice on fiction; Brian O'Riordan; Myra Blackburn of Lever Brothers Inc., Toronto for material on Sunlight Park; Marty Gervais for his editorial advice and the hot dogs at Tiger Stadium; Steven and Carole Johnston; Joan Johnston; Provost R. Painter, Dean C.J. McDonough and Professor Derek Allen of Trinity College for the opportunity to research Crane; Professor Thomas Hull of Trinity College for his assistance with mathematical matters; the Fellows at High Table; and to the members of the Seneca Baseball Course. Thank you Rayanne.

I am especially indebted to Homer Meyer, Margaret Meyer, Dr. Carolyn Meyer and Kerry Johnston for their patience, their keen editorial eyes and their unfaltering support.

Thanks to all and keep cheering for the home team.

B.M.

Table of Contents

Horse Diving *(a prose poem)*	8
Calling Time	15
The Order	27
Long Way Up, Short Way Down	39
Sunlight Park	49
The Glove	66
Goodbye Mr. Spalding	75
The Death of Grass *(a poem)*	95
The Summer Is Over	97
Father	110

*Here's the pitch. He swings! Long fly ball!
That's back! Goodbye Mr. Spalding!*

> home run call from the film version
> of "The Natural" (1984)

Horse Diving
(*a prose poem*)

Babe was only the name for a small child and a sultan was a Turk who kept women in a harem when the white stallion first leapt from the scaffolding and disappeared beneath the green waters of the bay. The men cheered. The women gasped and the young girls held their breath for the few moments that the equine head vanished beneath the waves.

And when the white muzzle broke the surface like an iceberg severed from a cool and distant glacier, there was a round of applause that pealed in volleys of enthusiasm, reminding the throngs of gunfire and thin red lines and union jacks fluttering in an offshore breeze on the glorious first of July.

Later that night, as the crowd elbowed and jostled for a spot on the shoreline just beyond the rollercoaster, a tall old lady of the lake burned at her mooring in a great bellow of flame, and the orange and yellow and greenish twists spiralled into the grey smokey extravaganza that rose up to the stars in an offering of summer joy. Its spars spread like the arms of a martyred saint, and hissed and spat like a cranky old crone as she slid to the muddy bottom of Algonquin Bite, charred black as the sky. The crowd turned away to their cottages or the ferries that bore them through the slumbering silences of a humid Toronto night.

The white stallion's name was Goliath and he was billed as the greatest thrill in the City of Toronto, King of Centre Island and Emperor of Summer. Each day the powerful beast would mount his scaffold like a condemned prisoner, hesistate for a moment atop his vantage point, perhaps peruse the steeples and chimneytops of the city across the harbour, before taking his headlong plunge into the tepid waters of the bay. Such power. Such a beast. Goliath was the feature attraction of the Island, and next to the great merry go-round, each figure hand-carved with care and detail in a Phildelphia factory, the most beloved thing of the lagoons and channels in the city's sidereal territories. Not even the stadium beyond the merry-go-round could compete with the star attraction.

After the fire a few years earlier the old Diamond Park had been replaced by the new Maple Leaf Park, a symbol of national pride and sportsmanly excellence, heralded throughout the Dominion for its covered stands and cooling bayside breezes to fan even those most passionate enthusiasts. The sun shone through the cracks and pores of the pine plank outfield fence, and in its canopied concrete tiers, which surrounded the grassy field of almost perfect green, was heard the majestic voice of championship the year the *Titanic* was lost.

But for those who had glimpsed the rising new palaces of the summer pastime south of the border, there was something almost delicate about the tiny island grounds at Hanlan's Point, something less than awe-inspiring for those who came to the islands to spend their time and their money to escape the awful heat which stalked the streets of the city like a hungry bengal. And for all its delicacy, the island park was simply another step in an endless procession toward forumly perfection, replacing an older rickety structure on the same site, and before that and further back than most observers of the game could remember, a patchy piece of raw ground known as Baseball Place on a lot that overlooked the flats below Broadview, the soap-works, and the brickworks chimneys of the Don Valley where a lazy brown river emptied into Goliath's daily dip and caused the great white horse to rise from the waters, on some days, a palid earthen hue.

Goliath was King, the stuff of legends. His rule was supreme. In the dry and pleasant days of July, the wonder horse was the talk of the city. His owner paraded up and down Yonge Street, the mighty beast on a leash. The ghostly shape of the white stallion, almost the size of a Clydesdale some said, cleared a path among the cart ponies, the draught horses and their wagons, and even the sombre black boxes of the horseless carriages. The town had something to talk about.

By Exhibition time during that last glorious summer of an era of summers, as the children tired of their vacation freedom and mothers tired of their children, Goliath had become a household word. His name became so familiar that even preachers mentioned it from the stern heights of their Presbyterian seriousness, and his name echoed in the consecrated rafters of gothic ceilings from one end of the city to the other, from the spire of Cook's in the east to the impregnable walls of Royce Victoria in the west. Parents were warned that too much of this giant was a bad thing for children; and the children, knowing it may be bad for them, loved him all the more.

To some children the beast became mythical. In their dreams it grew wings. It rose above the treetops and roofcrests and cast its mighty shadow on the streets below. Even the adults, who rarely lifted their imaginations above the daily consequence of bread and shelter, saw the horse as a kind of modern-day Pegasus, and they too felt young again in that heart-stopping moment when the equine shape took flight and shook his legs against a power of gravity only slightly greater than himself.

And when a shot rang out somewhere in Europe and Toronto slept in the dead of a summer night, most did nothing more than stir slightly in their beds, perhaps dream of a flying horse, islands shimmering beyond the harbour's edge, and summer endlessly in front of them like life itself.

A Prince toppled onto his wife's lap, and with a second burst, the Princess crumpled to the the landau's floor. The parade had taken a wrong turn. A blue-green river ambled between the ancient houses of a quaint mountainous city. "You must live for our children," the Prince whispered, each consonant sputtered with tiny drops of blood.

"So far away," people remarked to each other as they leaned on the rail of the sidewheeler *Trillium* and the Islands drew closer. Union Jacks appeared on storefronts. Only the children kept faith with Goliath.

Goodbye, Mr. Spalding

The first Saturday in September began with a morning rain. Torontonians woke to a grey mist that wandered through their streets, lost and confused, yet dense and refusing to lift as the sun struggled to break through in a last gasp of summer might.

"What does 'mobilization' mean?" children asked. The Prime Minister issued a proclamation.

A young man had knocked at the cottage door of a woman who had been his paddling companion all summer through the quiet lagoons and twisting channels of the islands. The dawn had not yet broken. He excused his impropriety. "I'm going to guard the coast," he said.

"Don't fall off," she replied and blushingly, yet groggy with disshevelled sleep, closed the door on her beau. She never saw him alive again.

As the *Trillium* paddled its way toward the island and the diving tower loomed above Hanlan's Point and cast an elongated shadow upon the ballpark's right field below, some talked anxiously of the events and bent in groups over *The Daily Star*. Others talked of what they had seen in the darkness the night before. A bright comet had crossed the sky. "You could read by it for an instant," said one man. Another shook his head. "It bodes poorly for princes, these things."

But those who were headed to the island for a final summer Saturday of carefree diversion paid no attention to the naysayers and gloom-mongers who carried the world of the city with them to the islands of forgetful bliss.

Today they would watch a baseball game. A team from Providence was in town. The Red Sox were taking a long look at a young kid from Baltimore whose pitching exploits had already made him the stuff of rumours.

They bought their tickets for twenty-five cents and filed into the little covered stadium. Those who arrived early had the best view of the field, partly high up in the in-field bleachers, and could look across the outfield to Goliath's tower. For the price of admission to the game, they figured, they could watch the Providential kid and the Mighty King, Goliath.

"He's got a kiddy woman's name," someone yelled before the first pitch had been thrown out by the Rhode Island team, and the crowd broke into laughter. The large bulk of the boy-child ambled toward the mound, his feet shuffling, his great rounded shoulders almost bent beneath the weight of the afternoon sun.

The taunts flew. Toronto was in first place tied with the Red Stockings. "Baby needs his Mommy!" Another roar of laughter went up. The first pitch of the game. A strike. The second. A strike. The third. The batter sat down. The crowd went quiet. The sun grew hotter. The pitcher walked back to the dugout, taller, more erect. His face was glowing.

By the sixth inning, Providence was up by a run. The young visiting pitcher had no-hit the Toronto side through four, and only then, did the Catcher, Billy Kelley, manage to single off a high and inside fastball that the rookie pitcher fired as a warning shot to those who wanted too much of the precious plate.

But two thirds of the way to a complete game, the visitors began to take charge. The crowd grew hushed. A pair of singles had been the difference. The Toronto pitcher was tiring. The sixth could have drawn to a close there and then leaving two men on and killing the morale of the zealous challengers. But the large, ambling youth who had pitched a good game so far and struck out twice with wild, broad, fanning swings, the swoosh and cut being heard almost a mile away, some said, came to the plate. He was grinning.

The first pitch was a strike. The crowd cheered. The second, low and inside, was swung at. Laughter broke out again. The umpire called time.

The boy batter leaned his weight on the knob of his bat and even slightly bent seemed to tower over the plate official and the catcher. The umpire looked toward the right field fence and shadowed his eyes against the glaring afternoon sun. A proud silouette cast its shadow on the field.

Goliath had been raised upon the scaffold. The crowd rose to its feet and cheered. The batter stood in the box, swinging, grunting like a wild beast and furrowing his brow into a deep and blackening rage. Had they come to see baseball or a horseshow? But the pitcher had turned to watch the spectacle that loomed over the outfield wall.

"Hey batter," yelled a voice from the stands. "Hold up and make way for the King of the Lake." The batter fixed his gaze on the outfield. The white beast cowered on the edge of the precipice. "Now!" roared the batter at the umpire, and startled the official who, almost apologetically, stepped back into his place behind the standing catcher who he tapped on the shoulder. "Play ball," called the ump. The catcher knelt, but his eyes were fixed almost worshipfully on the horse.

The pitcher heard the call, and turned to face his opponent. The crowd still set their gaze on the horse. A band played "A Minstrel Boy" behind the outfield fence.

The white beast reared its head high in a gesture of proud and sublime command. A cloud passed over the sun and for an instant the field darkened and then lightened again, suddenly, like an eye blinking in disbelief.

The pitch. The ball spun and twisted through the air. Hind legs reared up toward the emerging light.

The batter roared as if a great explosion erupted inside his soul.

Hooves lost contact with the platform and kicked out wildly at the ghost of an invisible enemy.

The crowd's mouths were open, but as in a dream, the shout did not come out. A crack followed a split second after the ball made contact with the ash. The shot climbed in an arc toward the leaping wonder. Eyes grew wider. The silence was breathtaking.

A small greyish sphere lifted into the heavens. Its stitches spun and twisted like a tiny world in agony, rising, out of control, headed for someplace beyond the imagination. It climbed and climbed as if it would never stop.

The white beast's legs pranced madly at the open air as if it were searching for a place and a time it could no longer find, a certainty that had become lost in the absurdity of the moment. And down, down it fell, rearing its head with a snarling pride, its white tail trailing behind it like a comet.

The ball sank from sight over the horizon of the wooden fence. And the young batter raised his hands as the bases cleared before him. One foot touched the plate, its cleat spraying an ether of dust into the air with a thunder that sounded in the hearts of those who watched like a death knell for first place and the aspirations of every daydreaming child. Another foot stomped in a run. The dust swirled in smokey cloud above the bag as the umpire signalled the score. And finally, triumphant with his arms raised, the batter moved like a locomotive down the alley from third to home.

"I am King of the Lake now," shouted Babe Ruth. "I am the King," he roared up to the stands as the crowd watched in disbelieving awe and a little boy shook his head and mouthed the word "no."

And as Ruth's cleated shoe touched the undeniable safety of home plate and the man on the scoreboard's catwalk reached for his stack of numbers only to knock them fluttering like lost birds into the crowd below, the great white beast who had been the idol of a dying summer, the last halcyon moments of a fading era, plunged beneath the green and churning waters of the bay, and was never seen again.

Calling Time

For years now I've had one wish: to finish our final game. Something inside says, "what if...what if." And if this world was only made of boyish dreams and baseball, we would have put our names on something to remember and be remembered for. "God," I say at night as I almost pray, "give me one more chance. Give me and the Kid a shot at finishing that last game."

He looked so young that dusty afternoon in Salinas when he stood tall in his first showdown. That was one helluva scorcher. The sun had no mercy. You could feel the desert thirst crying out through every pore of your skin. The bullets were flying. The outfield was a regular badlands. Bleached bones. Lost hopes.

We played way out west in the Sunset League. That was back in the late Forties. Class C. They called it the Sunset League not because of any post-card dusks or happy endings where the hero rides off into the after glow; for many it was the end of the line while for others it was the start of the long road with a faint glimmer of hope shining like a brass ring at the end of the tunnel, a lone star more distant than the eye could see, and the word "Majors" hanging there before them like the Holy Grail. A lot of the guys had gone west after the war to find their fortunes -- spot players who had filled in for the Dimaggios and the Williamses who were off doing real things in real places.

I'd gone west on a hunch. The majors had filled up with all the hotshots returning from active service. I was a real lonesome cowboy. No wife, no job, not much of a record even at the minor league level. I wasn't even much of a soldier. I never made it farther than an Uncle

Sam dirt camp in Louisiana and that for just six months toward the end. I'd come up in those sweaty south-eastern leagues where a man can earn more hauling sacks of grain for an hour than tearing grass with cleated shoes. Someone in a bar one night told me there was money to be made out west in some new operation called The Sunset League. I liked the name.

I ended up in this dusty little town called Las Vegas, a place that was really nothing in the middle of nowhere back then. I was one of the "Wranglers," and was battery mate to some strange hurlers; but in those days it was like the old saying "catch as catch can." Old gunslingers. New bucks. You hate to watch them go down and you can't bear to watch them come up.

So, there I was that afternoon, sifting for diamonds in the dust of homeplate and picking strikes out of the dirt. The sun was so hot and unforgiving you just hoped we'd bat through the order every inning just to spend longer in the dugout where it wasn't much cooler, but where we had shade, at least. But we didn't. Our order wasn't that heavy.

Our main arm, our town marshall...and I always want to go calling him Roy Bean, but that wasn't his name... a guy named Roy Banton who'd kicked around the Texas Leagues for a dog's age and finally got a shot at our club during a losing streak in June, got roughed up pretty bad in the early going of a shoot-out.

You could tell by the look on his face that Bean just wanted to catch the first stage out of there. So our Manager, more as an act of mercy than as a matter of strategy, leans over and in the ear of the Pitching Coach whispers to him like he's a counsel at a Senate hearing and points down the bench to this young buck who'd just ridden in that morning from hell-knows-where. And Old Roy is a has-bean.

As the Coach is making his way out to the mound, I sort of waddle out from the box, taking my time, because as I said it's damn hot. Damn, damn hot. And the Coach taps his left arm and that's how it all started, our working relationship. Me and The Kid.

This 'Kid' sprints some warmup in the bullpen as if he's sent from God with a message of joy. This big smile is spread across his face because he knew something none of us knew about what he was going to do. He sticks out his hand to receive the ball while he's still a good forty feet from the hill. There he is, running with his left hand out. Gimme, gimme. He wanted it alright. He looked like some kinda trophy running along out there.

The Coach simply nodded. No word. He just nodded. And the Kid turns the ball over and over in his hands like he's never seen one before, so I figured I'd better say something to break the ice because we hadn't exactly practiced together, so all the symbiotic stuff that you usually want to have between a pitcher and catcher just wasn't there.

I looked him in the eye, gave him that desperate look and said "You're town Marshall now and it's high noon." And I added, "by the way, I'm McKerrow," and the Kid turns to me, still smiling, and he says back, "and I'm good." Just like that; "and I'm good." And dammed if he wasn't.

He grins and starts talking in this put-on cowboy voice "No bad guys are gunna keep me from my wedding day," and I'd swear I heard Gary Cooper's voice come out of his mouth. This Kid walked into a shooting gallery and he knew it. At this point, I'm thinking, "this is *High Noon*." The bases are loaded, no one out, seventh inning and we're down by three runs, so what does he do? He sets them down in order. Boom, boom, boom. There he was, standing tall beneath that criminal sun, his cheeks all smooth and white, a hard afternoon light slapping him around that would have made any other man pay for being out there; but not him.

"Kid," I said, "are there any more like you back home?" And he just shakes his head. There sure weren't any like him where I'm from. Maybe none anywhere.

By the time our road trip was over, we'd gone all the way from fifth to third on the strength of the Kid's arm. I sat one night in one of those new boomtown saloons that were beginning to sprout out of the Nevada desert. The place was all coral and turquoise and chrome, and the curved naugahyde booths wrapped around the room like waves on a beach. A big neon sign flashing "Cocktails, Cocktails" on and off and on again lit up the night sky with a sparkling arrow pointing to the parking lot entrance where white Cadillacs shone orange and yellow beneath the glittering glare.

Money was coming out of the sky in that place. Boomtown. And for a ball player who was earning a capped salary of twenty-eight hundred a year, the sparkle was all the harder to believe. Everyone wanted a piece of the action. And somehow, something inside me kept saying, "this is all a mirage, you've seen this all before." That's the story of the wild west. The towns come and go. And if you sink a dollar or your heart into one place you're bound to be eating tumbleweed in six months. I guess I was wrong about Vegas.

The Kid strode in from a big white Cadillac that had pulled up out front. He was wearing a white suit with broad silk lapels and a bright green tie with a palmy oasis painted across it. "How you doing, Kid?" I asked him over my beer.

He ordered a martini because that's what the young bucks in white suits were drinking in those days, a drink that hollered out to everyone in the joint that you were a success if you asked for it in the right kind of voice. He had that big stupid grin on his face like he had that first afternoon as he strode to the mound.

"I've just been talking to some big shots from a team in Hollywood. Pacific Coast League. Ya' know Dimaggio and Williams played that circuit? And Stengel. Stengel's there in Oakland."

"So they read the sports page."

"No, no, this was real. This wasn't jus' some mirage outta the desert. This was real. They're talking to me."

"Kid," I said, "they got better places to look for the next saviour of the Spalding cause than out here in the middle of nowhere. Did they talk contract? Have they got paper? Did they name a figure?"

"Well, no," was the answer. There were times when I thought the Kid was a bit of a hayseed. "No, they didn't say anything about a contract. But they kept saying they were from Hollywood. The Stars, you know. That's halfway to the big time."

"Did they show you any credentials? You know how some folks like to pull the legs of ball players."

"C'mon, McKerrow. Whaddya take me for? Geez." He looked disgusted, like I was trying to betray him or something, and he stared into his drink. All I wanted to do was to set him right. There are people who will pull the legs of ball players, and any other strings they can manage to get their fingers on.

There was this one fellow in the Cottons, years ago when the going was tough as hell in the Thirties. His name was Fisher. Fisher could catch. If it was round and airborne, he was your man. But *they*, and I don't know who *they* were, *they* got to him. The Slicks. The money men. They got to him.

And one day when our championship was on the line, Fisher turned into an open window behind the plate. Everything flew out. And for a catcher that's the kiss of death, and I couldn't understand. Couldn't understand a thought of it until I glanced out my hotel room window and saw Fisher going off in a big dark car in the middle of the night. That's when I got the picture.

Everything was kept hush about that final game because the last thing you want in a measly league is a dark cloud hanging over a half-empty stand. But I heard later that Fisher turned up again, somewhere in the midwest, and the next time he got caught. That's sacrilege, not just because you break the law, but because you break the code of the game and the hearts of all the guys you play with and against. You can't be trusted anymore. Everyone knows you aren't clean. And if a ballplayer's got anything at all in this world, when all is said and done, it's his clean. Lose that, especially among your peers, and you're nothing.

And I saw the Kid sitting there and I just knew someone had promised him the rainbow. And I said, "Kid live *your* life. Live clean." But at that age, when you're good, any offer that sounds better is a promise. And Las Vegas in 1947 was a land of promises. "Be careful," I warned.

We were heading back to a block of low, pink, adobe apartments where some of the players lived, when a pale blue Packard came flying out of nowhere and ambushed our taxi. I was knocked unconscious. The cab burst into flames. The police told me that the Kid had pulled the cabbie and me from the flaming wreckage.

I remember lying there in dust as I came to, and the Kid was standing over me and the stars were ringing round his head and dancing inside mine. The flames from the burning vehicle threw an orange glow on his face. "You saved my life," I said.

He just smiled and shrugged and brushed the dirt off that white suit of his. That was when I knew the Kid was a hero, not just your everyday hero, but the storybook kind — white suit, white horse, and an orange sunset behind him in the distance just waiting for him to ride off into.

A week later we were out of town again. We headed further into the desert. We took the trail to Reno. They were called the Silversox. Their uniforms were silver and black and they were the meanest bunch of hombres west of the Rio Grande.

The season was drawing to a close and we still had a shot at the pennant. Every game mattered. Every hit mattered. When you push a bunch of old horses hard they show every step of the trail. You could see the strain on the faces in the dressing room. You could look into the corners of a man's eyes and count the drives he'd been on. The seasons of their careers were etched like dried riverbeds around the corners of their mouths where sweetheart smiles used to shine. These were hardened men; these also were tired men.

The Kid was hot, though. He'd set the league on fire and everyone was talking about him. He'd cleaned up in one town after another. He was in tight in the race for most wins with a fella named Frank Miller who played for Reno -- a big mean pitcher who thought he owned the plate and who would gun down any man who thought differently.

We won the first game in Reno. It was tight. In the seventh, the Kid walked two. I went out to the mound to have a chat.

"You're starting to miss. They're spotting you on the corners."

"Yeah," he said, removing his cap and wiping the sweat off his brow. "I'm having trouble thinking. There are some guests here today." He pointed to the third row just left of the screen. There were some Slicks in silk suits and dark glasses.

"Ignore them," I said, "you're playing, they're only watching. Inside tight on the next one. Got it?" The Kid nodded. We pulled it out with a bunt single in the ninth and a man on third.

I sat alone in the locker room after the game. My body was beginning to catch up with me. The summers were growing longer, even then. I liked being the last to leave, the silence, the feeling of just being able to sit there and hear nothing, yet still smell the game and the grass on the cleats of my shoes. I would wander through the empty corridors of the stadium and all around me sense the bulk of a huge beast that had suddenly been brought down with a mighty blow. And that's when I overheard the conversation: the Kid and the Slicks.

"We've put a great deal of capital into this venture. Some very impressive people have financial interests in a certain team, not your own, becoming champions at the end of the schedule."

"So," said the Kid. "What's that got to do with me?"

"They've got you scheduled to pitch the day after tomorrow. It would be in your best interests to do a very poor job for your team. The compensation would greatly enhance your financial situation. Our friends in L.A. would notice your fine record and ignore one bad day."

"No. I'm clean. I'm staying clean. That's all I got to say." The Kid turned and started to walk away. I heard the noise of a scuffle and I was ready to step in.

"You damned little sonnuvabitch. You think you're above everyone and everything in this piss-ass little league? Well, you're not. You throw your next game or we kick the shit out of you. Better still, you're friends with the Catcher...what's-his-name...McKerrow. Yeah. McKerrow. You lose the day after tomorrow or we'll break both of McKerrow's legs, and maybe your pitching arm as well." I heard a punch being thrown and I raced around the corner. The Slicks were through the gate. A big white Cadillac was pulling away. The Kid was doubled over against the wall.

"Kid," I asked, "you alright? Did they hurt you?" He nodded. "Who were those jerks?"

"Hollywood," said the Kid. "Those were the guys who were talking Hollywood back in Vegas. They aren't from a team. They're gamblers. I owe them some money." I helped the Kid to his feet and brushed the dirt off his arm.

"How much?"

"Fifteen grand."

21

"Shit, Kid." The words just hung there in my mouth. "Look, we got to go to the management. We got to tell them what you're in for." He stared at me incredulously.

"Do you think I'd ever play ball again, anywhere, if they found out I was in with gamblers?" He had a point. I drew in my breath.

"How much did you hear, Mac?"

"I heard enough, Kid, but I ain't afraid of them. They're just full of shit. You stay clean. You understand me."

"Mac, I saw them beat the hell out of a guy because he didn't have a grand he owed them. A measly grand. I'm in for fifteen times that. They're betting on Reno for the pennant. But they aren't going to do anything until the day after tomorrow. I'll think of something by then."

The hours passed slowly. The Kid and I waited it out. He paced back and forth across carpet of the motel where the team was staying. He stared out the drapes at a big white Cadillac that sat parked at the edge of the lot. "They aren't ready to make their move yet," he said.

Game time came. We strode out of the dugout together. The sun was blazing directly above. A strange hush hung over the crowd. This was the showdown. Miller was pitching for Reno. The Kid was our gunner. The Slicks were in their seats. Watching. They had come to see their dreams come true. So had the Kid.

In the first, the Kid set the side down on straight strikes. He did it again in the second and in the third. Miller allowed two runs. The Slicks were adjusting their collars. In the fourth, the Kid walked out alone to the mound. He was standing tall. And suddenly, a strange look came over the Kid's face. One of the Slicks had stood up in his seat and was pointing at homeplate. At me.

The Kid looked at the Slick and shook his head as if he was shaking off a signal. The sky silvered over and began to darken. The Kid just stood there, staring down the pike, the batter waiting. The umpire called time. I ran out to the mound.

"What's wrong?"

"I'm waiting," the Kid replied.

"For?"

"For the rain. Any minute." He cocked an eye to the sky. "Its going to rain one helluva desert rain. A once-in-a-century gush. It's going to wash our sins away. I'll still be clean. We'll all be clean." I backed up toward the mound and pulled my mask down. The Kid hollered, "just you watch, McKerrow. Just you watch. You'll know what to do." And as I crouched behind the plate and the batter stepped in, I really didn't know what was going to happen. I saw the Kid out there, trapped like a mustang in a blind canyon, with no way out except a miracle. And then it happened.

The sky split open like it had been holding back all the oceans of the world. It poured and poured and sent the Slicks scattering for cover from their seats. And the Kid just stood there on the mound, still clutching the ball, holding it tightly and staring into the zone. He went into his wind-up, but the batter could hardly see him for the torrent, and through the greyish haze of the falling rain, as the desert itself almost seemed to be washed away beneath the heavenly barrage, came the ball spinning and hurtling and cannonading faster than I'd ever seen anything thrown in my life. And when it hit my glove, it resounded with an echoing pock. A strike.

The batter stepped from the box and stared at his bat. I craned my neck around and stared up at the official. He raised his palms as if he was a preacher announcing a benediction on a holy moment and hollered "Time!" then ran for the Reno dugout as he turned his collar up. And as I stood there in the box with that river of mercy pouring down upon me, I saw the Kid on the mound, laughing and laughing as the rain swallowed him in its shroud.

It rained for seven hours. The Slicks waited beneath the stands. Our team waited in the clubhouse. And finally, just as the sun was setting, the downpour stopped. The clouds parted and the sky turned orange like the backdrop for a hero. The Umpire announced that we'd complete the game tomorrow ahead of the final set-to of the season.

And when the Slicks went to the parking lot to find their white Cadillac, they found it was gone, hot-wired by someone, the police said, when they found it several states away with a baseball on the seat and the word "adios" written on a tiny note. No one could find the Kid.

Frank Miller won the pitching title for the Sunset League that season on virtue of his start the next day in the final game. Coming so close was hard for our team, but the veterans had seen it all before. I believe that if the Kid had finished that penultimate game, he would have walked off with the hurler's crown, and perhaps had that shot at the big-time he had always wanted. But he had other things on his mind.

When I saw the Kid had hit the road, I immediately went to the Management and told them that the Slicks had been hanging around. And when the gamblers arrived at the motel that evening to pay me their regards, bats in hand of course, the police were waiting for them.

But the Kid never realized just how close he'd come. Or perhaps he did. At least he had some control over who ended his career. Management took a dimmer view of my role in the whole thing. I wasn't all that upset, though. I'd had a good run. I'd played my game. All but one game, of course.

I kept looking for his name to turn up in *The Sporting News* or *The Spalding Guide*, but no luck. I suppose he just jumped in that big white Cadillac, hit the road and kept right on going until flooded highways and a blown gasket signalled the end of the Kid's trail on the outskirts of Houston. That's the nature of drifters; they don't leave trails if they don't have to.

The old league is gone now. Eventually the Sunset faded to black via the transformation of the most poetic name ever given to a circuit into a handle of a more prosaic ilk: the Southwest International League.

When I get talking to some of the fans at Chavez Ravine, I ask them if they ever heard of Class C ball being played in these parts, and for the life of them they haven't a clue what I'm talking about. Most of the parks were ploughed under for real-estate. One, the old park in Reno, is now the site of a used car lot. I passed by there one day about ten years ago when I had some business in the city of divorce, and there under the banners and coloured flags and strings of pastel electric lights was this old white Cadillac from the Forties, still shining, still just like new with all its chrome sparkling. And I thought of the Kid.

I've been searching for the Kid for years now. For my jobs I've Greyhounded from the southwest to the northeast and read every phone book along the way. There've been letters and phone calls and a few contacts with those who knew him or think they saw him.

Some say he played in South America. The Golden Gringo they called him there. Chile or some place. He got in a fight one night with someone who wanted him to throw a game he knew he could win, and that he died in the arms of some snazzy tango dancer with a knife thrust into his side.

Others claim he worked the wells in Texas after giving up the game before heading north to Canada to lay pipeline somewhere, and he pitched a perfect game beneath the midnight sun. That's what becomes of legends: more legends.

Something deep down inside tells me the Kid is still alive, still out there, somewhere, and maybe he's still got his stuff. That would be a joke on time. Heroes don't just ride off into the sunset. I know someday, somewhere, we will finish that last game. I will flash the signs. He will shake off some and ask for more. Right down the pike. Hard and fast. Gunsmoke.

The last, unfinished inning sticks in my mind. The rain is falling on his shoulders, his cap glistening with drops of silver light. The batter steps from the box. The pitch was a strike, a hard, emphatic fast ball. The Kid has more where that comes from. The batter examines his bat as if he is trying to get it to tell him a secret as tiny beads of mysterious desert gold roll down the white ash like tears from the eyes of a sorrowful Madonna.

I look to the mound and the Kid knows this is it, that our trail has come to the end. He gives me a glance with that silly grin of his, a grin that both trusts and knows, the look of certainty possessed by geniuses and fools. The Umpire steps out of the box and yells "Time." A crash of thunder fills the air. Eternity presides over the park. My lifetime catches up with me.

The Ump looks at the sky. He is a priest auguring a change in the universe. The cowboys are passing from the world. And a moment later the game is called. I begin to walk back to the dugout, but there behind me, as I turn and look at the vacant field, is the Kid, refusing to relinquish the mound. He stands on the rise, solitary as an enigmatic mountain in an otherwise empty landscape. No horse. No sunset. Just clean. Clean white.

I'm an old man now, but for me the Kid is still a kid. Legends never grow old. How young he looked, I mutter to myself as I recall him striding to the mound with his hand out. Gimme, gimme.

For me, the final inning is just around the corner, but I'm not afraid anymore. I know who the umpire is. I know what he is going to call.

And the Kid is saving his best stuff for last.

The Order

The November sun had yet to rise over Cartagena when shortstop Juan Toledo woke to the summoning of a restless dream. He had been in a bar the night before. That much was clear. A man's stubby fingers wrapped around the neck of a tequila bottle poured more and more into a tiny shot glass. The room swam in his head like it wanted an Olympic record. "I can make you anything you want," Toledo remembered the voice had said.

"Then make me a major league short stop. The best in the majors."

"We could work on that," the voice of that ethereal memory said. "There are others for whom we've done the same and one or two of them are still around. There might be some delay, until they retire. You realize, of course, there is a price. You must be prepared to pay the price."

Who was that guy? Who made him the offer and what was the price? Toledo rose uneasily from his bed, his fleet-footed balance lost with the night before in the maze of shabby old colonial streets and the loud music that poured from the cantinas in tsunamies of deafening delight. The ceiling fan turned slowly. He opened the shutters of his room that faced onto a painted faux balcony in the Hotel of the Wandering Angels. A grey mist had scuttled in from the sea and the streets stank like back-alley rooms where dreams went to die.

He knew the smell. He had known it all his life in that tiny village where women did their washing from plastic bowls on their doorsteps and chickens ran amongst children in the streets. And in a sandlot within the shadow of the tiny mission church, he had learned to hit and field and dream of the day he would thank God for his chance to play in the World Series.

Bits of recent past began to reconstruct themselves in his mind. The man with the stubby fingers had sported a cream-coloured suit and a panama hat with a black band. Why could he not see the man's eyes? Sun glasses. The man had worn black-rimmed shades like Roy Orbison's, and the eyes behind seemed to tunnel darkly into the pale flesh of the man's sweaty head.

And the red-haired woman? Yes. There had been a red-haired woman. He remembered the smell of her perfume, her smooth white arms, round breasts and pink nipples, and her back arched beneath the strain of their passion. The indentation of her head marked the pillow next to his, and a strand of her long fiery hair curled like a question mark across the white case.

And on his glove hand, his right hand, at the tip of the middle finger, there was a small wound which began to pain him, a tiny lancing nick in the shape of an x.

As the morning sun burned off the fog around the stadium and the players changed for their workout, Toledo sat in the clubhouse and grew more and more uncertain of events from the night before.

"You got lucky, eh?" winked his roommate, Pedro Sanchez, at the next locker. "Nice woman. Big tits. Thank me for staying clear all night. Now you will really start to hit. Get out the cold Jones from your joints."

"Were you there? Did you see me?"

"Only in the bar. You got moves, babe, you got moves."

"What did I say?"

"You talked about deals. Yeah, that was it. Deals. Deals. Deals. How much money you're going to make. Big cars. Yeah, big, fast cars." A terrible look came over Toledo's face and he felt the blood draining out of him.

He had heard the old men of his village in the Dominican tell a legend about tequila. The souls of the damned are imprisoned in the agave cactus because there is no more room left in hell. They are released if the plant dies, but the usual fate of those damned in such a way is that they are juiced and fermented into the demon drink. A tequila drunk is like no other: the souls of the damned are consumed. The dreams are the lives of the damned being played out one last time as the drinker takes their salvation into his own soul and suffers their torments as if they were *his* life. "Yes," thought Toledo. "The man in the suit must have been a memory from the tequila."

The earthly torment of an afternoon game in the equatorial sun was pronounced upon them. Toledo threw to Sanchez at first base to end the opening inning. They always made the connection on the defence, and they made it look good. Both were young and wanted to be noticed. It was the only way up.

But lately Toledo's hitting had been poor, not as poor as Sanchez', but bad enough to drop him in the order all the way from clean-up to eighth, just ahead of Sanchez. The order remained that way all winter. Cartagena finished dead last. There wasn't much to take north to Florida.

On the eve of reporting day, Toledo sat drinking beer with Sanchez in an arborite tabled family restaurant off one of those thin little coastal highways, and their booth was lit by the glow that flooded through the window from the parking lot of the Piggly Wiggly across the thoroughfare.

"Pedro, I've got to get something off my chest."

"You are my buddy, you can share anything with me."

"Thank you," said Toledo as he looked down into his glass. He could see his palid reflection swimming on the surface of his drink where the foam had disappeared and his image was pierced by the San Sebastian arrows of the rising carbonation.

"You remember that night in Cartagena last November? The red haired woman?" Pedro nodded. "Well, it was strange what happened before she came back to the Wandering Angels. She was with a guy, right?"

"I can't remember," replied Pedro with a shrug. "You brought so many women back, I spent most of my nights sleeping at a friend's house."

"I've been trying to piece it all together. There was this guy in a pale suit. A gringo, sweating all over the place. And I couldn't see his eyes. The more I remember, the more...I don't know. God forgive me."

"What? What?" asked Sanchez. "You knocked her up? She wants money?"

"I think," said Toledo slowly, "I think I sold my soul for a shot at the majors. I think I sold off heaven and eternity and my very spirit to be the best in the game."

Pedro broke into a smile. The smile widened into a grin and the grin into uncontrollable laughter. "Cabrone! Make me laugh! You hit like shit. You'd be lucky this year to make Single A. Man we're both shit hitters. If they oozed a mountain of shit out of a molasses barrel we wouldn't be able to hit it with a truck! They aren't going to send us north. They gotta make money, not jokes. I see you hopping off the rural bus in that hill village above Azua and me getting off at the next stop. You're very funny when you're worried. You should be a poet or a philosopher. They worry all the time. You may be one sooner than you think."

Toledo shrugged. After a few more beers they gathered their courage and decided to face the inevitable by reporting the next morning for the team physicals.

By the third week of the Grapefruit schedule things were looking bleak. The big bonus rookies who had been drafted out of the colleges were getting more time in the cages, more attention from the instructors and more innings in the intrasquads. And then, something strange occurred.

They'd gone to play the Pirates at Clearwater in a split squad. The regular short-stop, a Gold Glove All-Star named Mancey, dove for a catch and landed on his elbow. The shattering pop could be heard all through the park, the slo-mo out through the skin was repeated on newscasts across the nation and at six and eleven.

Everyone felt bad for Mancey, especially Mancey who had just signed a four-year contract worth an estimated three million a season, because even as he landed on his elbow, as if time had slowed down to a frame-by-frame replay of something that had already happened, it was plain to see that this was the end of his career. "He had a lot more in him," everyone said; "but that's baseball." The Split-squad Manager, a base coach on the big club, looked down the bench and pointed to Toledo.

"Hit shit Juan," said Pedro as Toledo grabbed a bat from the rack and adjusted his helmet on the dugout steps. Pedro mimed a driving motion. And on the first pitch, as if by magic, the ball made a lovely connection. "Hello," said the bat to the ball; "Goodbye" said the ball as it cleared the outfield fence.

Sanchez, who was put in as a pinch-hitter, followed with a double, and suddenly the Pirates were out of the game. In the weeks that followed, Toledo went on a tear. The kid from nowhere stayed around after the college boys had been cut or whittled down to Class A. He stayed around after the Double A boys broke camp and headed to the farmlands of the Carolinas. And Sanchez was always right behind him, grinning and laughing at their accomplishments.

Toledo and Sanchez sat together as the team bus shuttled between Baseball City and Bradenton late in the Grapefruit schedule. "You know," said Sanchez, "they're talking Triple A. And then, who knows? The way you keep hitting, all that stands between you and the Cadillac is Rothstein."

Toledo shook his head. " Pedro, I know what the score is. They're going to go with Rothstein. They've been grooming him for years. Shortstop of the future."

"Don't count on it, amigo. Don't count on it."

But the big club did open with Rothstein, and for the first few weeks Rothstein was passable to solid on defence. Everyone said the future phenom would settle in, that it was just a matter of time for the rookie for whom the club had waited so long. Rothstein was destined to be the next Ripken. But Rothstein had one problem: he loved to take the plate. Anyone could see it when he batted. He would look down at the pentagon and everyone just knew the word "Mine" was going through his head as he cocked his bat and edged slowly over the zone. And the pitchers who had seen him in Triple A knew that they couldn't throw outside -- he reached for those. They had to pitch him down the pike or in tight. And that was how it happened. In tight. In San Diego.

Rothstein stepped up late in the third inning. The Padres had a monster named Bowley they'd raised from the depths of Single A. Bowley threw heat. Hard heat. Outside heat. Wild heat.

Rothstein saw bait. He leaned gently over the plate as the pitch left the mound looking as if it was searching for a new zip code on the outside. Rothstein didn't even swing when suddenly the ball seemed to make an impossible ninety-degree turn at a sharp, inclining angle. The *in your face* became *between your eyes*.

"There was definitely something extra on that one!" cried the play-by-play man in the booth as Rothstein lay crumpled on the ground. "I haven't seen anyone take a shot like that since Peter Reiser in the 40s." The crowd hushed. Bowley's pitch made *This Week In Baseball*, and before he was sent back down, "to work on his control," Bowley also managed to bag a ball boy and the water cooler in the visitors' dugout.

Rothstein awoke three days later, absolutely sure he was an insurance salesman from Winnipeg named McDonald. "Wendy," he said as anxious press and team officials gathered around his bed to catch his first waking words, "how are we going to pay the mortgage?"

Rothstein's unexpected sojourn was poorly timed for the big club. The club was running tight with the Mets and the Shea Stadium gang were due in town for a four game stand. Toledo had gone cold in Triple A, and the big club had dealt away their utility infielder for a left-handed middle man who couldn't even relieve himself.

The brass huddled. Should they deal a pitcher and some prospects for a veteran shortstop? "That Dominican kid wasn't all he was cracked up to be," someone pointed out, "and his recent skid against good pitching wouldn't endear him even to an expansion franchise."

"A move like that would signal panic. Panic is the one thing another team shouldn't smell when talking trade. They'd burn us and we'd seem grateful."

"Are there any free agent hold outs we could sign?"

"They all want too much money."

"That isn't the route. The field is bleak."

Sweat began to pour from the foreheads of the team think-tank.

The base coach put in his two cents: "The kid hit fine for me in split-squads down south. He's clutch. He's better than nothing."

Nothing was not good the rear-admirals agreed, and neither was a guy who'd gone from sandlot to the majors in eight months, but something had to be done. Toledo it would be, as long as Rothstein was on the DL.

And so, Toledo arrived to fill the hole at short and Sanchez, right behind him, was brought up for insurance, utility, and pinch running.

That night in the hotel room, Juan Toledo wept inconsolably. Sanchez tried to comfort him. "Man, we're in the show. You should be happy. Look at me." Sanchez was smiling, showing all his teeth. "See? I'm happy. Really happy."

"But I've lost my soul. I've sold off God and grace and eternity for this room at the Sheraton and a chance to crash and burn in front of millions of people. I who was named for St. John of the Cross by my mother, God rest her soul, who was the most devout woman since the last beloved saint graced our fallen state. What will my mother say when I die and don't show up in heaven? She will grieve so much. It will break the heart of her soul. I don't know. It is all too real. I don't know what will happen."

"Okay, Juan. So let it happen. You're here. You can't change that. You claim you sold your soul to that representative of hell in the cream-coloured suit and Roy Orbison glasses. So, you can't change that either. So what do you do? You go out and hit. You hit hard and far. You run. You run fast. You catch. Man, you do those things, you play your game the way they taught us in the hills above Azua and you are an instant legend. Immortal. You live forever in the minds of the baseball fans. And all I can tell you is that no priest has ever been able to convince me there's any more of heaven than what exists in people's minds. So man, you're in heaven. You make the bigs, you live forever in people's minds."

Sanchez grabbed the sports section of the local newspaper and held it out unfolded for Toledo to see. "See this? This is a sign from some higher power that you have arrived." The picture on the front page of the section showed a grim looking Toledo arriving at the clubhouse door. Behind him was Sanchez, smiling. The headline:

Dominicans to the Rescue.

The announcer and the colour commentator were not overly kind the next day as Toledo warmed up in the on-deck circle and the crowd groaned as the outfielder Tolley got caught looking at pitches as slow and hitable as beachballs. All over the city car radios and transistors crackled with the AM sound of the play by play:

"*Up next in the ninth spot is that kid from the islands, Juan Toledo, who's filling in for Rothstein on the DL. Only a .210 on the farm and this club could use some heavy hitting right now. Tolley sits down on an off-speed. You can hear the crowd getting on him. Not like last season.*"

"*That's right Earl, he looked at some good stuff up there. He needs to cut down on his swing, or maybe he's swinging too late or too early or maybe...*"

"*Thanks Mike for that...*" The murmurs of the crowd could be heard in the background. "*Toledo called up yesterday with another Dominican, Pedro Sanchez hitting just .209 down there behind shortstop Toledo, and we'll probably only see Sanchez in pinch-running situations, if at all. There's the swing on a fastball for a strike. And you'd think, Mike, that this club seems almost ripe for a trade, and perhaps this new guy is simply here for showcasing. You've got to wonder.*"

"*He definitely could be trade bait. He's young and could develop some potential, but as for being major league material, well, its out of any power in this world to say, that's for sure.*"

"*The pitch. Holy cow! Has he connected! That ball is still rising! Going, going, gone! Homerun for the new rookie sensation from the farm! Holy Toledo! Did that thing get wood on it!*"

The crowd was screaming. The scoreboard lit up JUAN-DER-FUL!!! Fireworks exploded.

After the game, a win on a Toledo three run shot, the two Dominicans huddled together, wrapped in towels, in a corner of the clubhouse. Sanchez was smiling. Toledo, still grim-faced, was fielding questions. All he could manage in English was "Bass-bull be bery bery goo tuh me."

That night, in their room at the Sheraton they watched Telelatino with the sound off. Sanchez put down a copy of the early edition.

"Hey Juan, see the headline in the paper? Right here. Tomorrow's edition. 'Rothstein who?' Pretty good, no?"

"Pedro, this can't be happening to me. I go four for four with two home runs, five RBI's and a stolen base and I can't hit shit. I'm frightened. I'm damned."

Pedro put his arm around his buddy to console him. "Let's go for a walk. You need to stretch your legs and clear your head. You're thinking crazy."

The two walked for several blocks through the empty streets. Juan Toledo felt very small and insignificant beneath the office towers and stone fronts. Sanchez revelled in the big city lights and seemed to dance along the street as he shouted "We're here, we're here."

Suddenly, a couple stepped from an alley way, and standing there in front of Toledo and Sanchez was the panama-hatted man in the cream-coloured suit and the sultry woman with the red hair.

The man looked directly at Sanchez. "No need for introductions. We know Mr. Toledo. Some game today, wasn't it? You were very very good. Much good bass-bull." He chuckled to himself as the two Dominicans exchanged uncomprehending glances. "This is going to be good for our deal. A real sweetner," exclaimed the gringo.

Toledo's eyes popped with terror and he began to shake uncontrollably. He started to cry "God help me, oh God help me. They've come to take me." Pedro attempted to silence his friend. The gringo turned to Sanchez.

"What's he shouting about, calm him down."

Sanchez tried to translate. "He yell at God. He say he take it. He say 'they come for me.'"

"On the contrary, we're here to do nothing of the kind. Allow me to explain," the man said as he straightened his tinted and impenetrable Roy Orbison glasses. The red-haired woman primped her coiffe. "What you did today was a remarkable demonstration, because, you must face it, you just can't do that kind of thing every day. Consider it a test drive. Just a taste of what is to come, if you are willing, so to speak, to play ball with us. Your name up in lights. The fans hollering and chanting for you. Promotions galore. I trust you have thought about the offer I made you in Cartagena."

35

The man turned to Sanchez. "Does your friend here understand a word of what I'm saying? *Comprenez?* Yes?" The man nodded at Toledo and Toledo, terrified, nodded back. "I am here to offer you baseball immortality in return for..."

With that Toledo turned and ran, shouting "No, no!" Pedro ran after him. The two didn't stop until they reached the Sheraton, and they sat up all night, silently watching Telelatino.

By afternoon the next day, another game was in full swing. Toledo, based on his stunning performance the day before, had moved up in the order from ninth to clean up. In the first he had hit a grand slam. The crowd chanted his name. In the fourth he had led off with a triple. Energy arched from the team bench. The atmosphere was electric. The Mets were toast. Sanchez watched from the bench, his smile still firmly in place.

But in the seventh, with one man on and none out, Toledo stopped his warm-up in the circle and turned to Sanchez on the bench.

"Last night," Toledo spoke in Spanish, "last night when we saw that man and woman from Cartagena, he knew you. He spoke to you and said he knew my name. He knew you, didn't he?" Sanchez shrugged. Toledo's name was announced. He stepped to the plate.

Sanchez tried to call after him "*delegado*", but his voice was drowned by the crowd.

The pitch came inside. A strike was called. The crowd silenced. Under his breath, Juan Toledo said a little prayer. "Father in Heaven, I would not trade eternity with you for anything. I am not like that. Forgive me my sins and help me to hit this ball."

The next pitch came inside, a slider, but with all his strength, a strength inside he had never felt before -- as if ten men pulled together in one mighty act -- he made contact with the ball. It rose over the head of the first baseman and dropped in just in front of the right-fielder who had been playing the heavy-hitter well back. The cut-off throw went to second to hold Toledo at first. "Holy Toledo," exclaimed the fans. Toledo stood at first, adjusted his gloves, straightened his helmet, and brushed some dirt off the shins of his white trousers. He looked back at the dug-out and glared at Sanchez.

The next batter came to the plate, and on a 2 and 0 outside pitch, Toledo took off. He ran and ran as fast as his legs could carry him.

He felt the wind parting on the crest of his face, and saw from the corner of his eye the catcher rise to his feet and release a bullet throw to second. Toledo lifted his legs from the ground and began his jet-like slide into the base.

A cloud of dust rose around his face blinding him, and in that instant he heard a tremendous crunch and felt a bolt of lightning rise along his right leg.

"Safe!" hollered the official. The dust thinned and choked him and seemed to reach into his nostrils to strangle his spirit.

The pain grew more and more intense and crept all the way up to his head where it tried to escape into the world as a scream; but he held it in, wanting somewhere deep inside him to contain and nurture this horrible monster that his leg had created. And with that, he passed out.

He saw the bus winding through the dense overgrowth of the tropical afternoon as it made its way up the hill to the little village where the women paused from their washing and the children and chickens ran to flee the path of the creaking vehicle as it groaned to a halt in the square. The bus door opened, and as he descended into a cloud of dust he paused for an instant on the steps and saw the blue-green hills shimmering in the pale humidity and the sun beating down on the stillness of landscape that stretched into the distance like a promise of forever. And he thought it odd that the door of the little white church was open at that time of day, and that the women were putting their washing aside and making their ways to worship in the heat of the afternoon. One of them called to him across the square as the bus pulled away, "Come with us. We will sing the Agnes Dei."

A low and almost silent murmuring rumbled through the stadium as Toledo opened his eyes. The trainers and ambulance men were lifting him onto the stretcher. Sanchez stood above him.

"Don't worry Juan, I'm running for you now. I'm playing short next inning too."

"You?" asked Toledo through the pain which had infiltrated every corner of his body.

"Yes," replied Sanchez softly. "I'm going to be immortal."

"Pedro, Pedro," pleaded Toledo, "You were there that night in Cartagena. Did I really sell my soul?"

"No, amigo," grinned Sanchez. "It was I who sold mine. My rise simply hastened you through the order. I am sorry for your pain. But man, I just know I'm going to Disneyland!"

And as they carried Juan Toledo off the field and the crowd rose in a round of thankful applause, the former shortstop for the big club, Holy Toledo, clasped his hands together in a gesture of prayer. Tears of joy that some saw as intense pain flowed from his eyes.

He stared adoringly into the perfectly endless blue heaven of that summer afternoon, relieved to know that he, Juan Toledo, who was named in holiness for St. John of the Cross and raised in faith by a devout and saintly mother, still had his place in God's loving heart among the believers, the innocent and the forgiven.

Long Way Up, Short Way Down

When the recurring nightmare got to him, when he felt it hanging over him like a slow pop fly, he junked around with ideas in his mind -- concepts from any absurd material at hand. Today the idea was mathematical, of sorts, that the shoddiness of the bus was proportional to the gaudiness of the minor league polyester uniforms. Bright baby blues. Sharp floral yellows. Startling never-crease reds. Graphed on a Cartesian plane where $y = mx + b$, and m is the slope (which inevitably sloped down), he was also able to conclude, although less evidently, that the number of crawling things in the motel linen was equivalent to the circumference of the gravelled parking lot, provided that the bus did not have room to turn. Or something like that.

Nights in those motels he would waken and hear the songs of nubile young checkout clerks from the nearest Montgomery Ward or Piggly-Wiggly experiencing ecstasy beneath the sweating hulks of local businessmen who were sure, absolutely sure when questioned by their wives, that they had left the bar an hour earlier but the car wouldn't start. "Only good thing about these dumps," he said one morning as his room-mate shaved, "is that you can open the windows and let some air get in."

As he considered the idea and its associated recollections, the smell of the bus made him sick. The bouncing motion turned his stomach. He had tried to read a book of Shakespeare's *Sonnets* someone had given him along the way. He couldn't remember who that was. "Enlarge your mind, son." Who the hell was that? Every line kept reminding him of something he'd experienced in his own life.

"When in disgrace with fortune and men's eyes, I all alone beweep my outcast state." Pure James Dean. Alone and beweeping and outcast state. The going was slow. The more he read, the sicker he felt, the more he remembered. "You shouldn't read on the bus. Bad for the eyes," his Manager told him. "You'll lose those short pop-ups." He nodded out of routine just so the guy would lay off him.

At the end of each game, he would scrape up a handful of earth from the batters box and carry it with him to the next park. Continuum. That's how you get a string going. If the smell of diesel got too much for him, he would rub the mud on his upper lip, inhale the earthy aroma of grit and sweat and ball, and pull his cowboy hat over his eyes and feign sleep. He would doze into semi-consciousness with the smell of either victory or defeat superimposed on the miles of "I" roads leading north and south and east and west in search of their own destination, a semi-sleep interrupted only by the tunnel, the light, the pain and the denial.

And there he was in the dream again, in the middle of a long corridor with a white light behind him and a darkness ahead. The sensation in the dream kept telling him that if he turned back toward the light he was going to feel incredible pain. A dull roaring always overscored the vision. For an instant he didn't know who he was or where he was. He was something, somebody else, an imagining from a once-upon-a-time daydream in his childhood that he could not locate in time, a faceless spectre into which he had knowingly cast himself, a shadow without past, present or future.

* * *

His teammates had nicknamed him 'Egg' in the Florida League; that's where you fry and die or crack and fly; that's where many embryonic careers go unhatched. And he'd scrambled a few plays which had not endeared him to his teammates. "Egg Brain," they said, but his detractors wouldn't find him inside his shell, fast asleep, dreaming of everything life had to offer -- everything except that damn tunnel. So, on the long trips between the parks he pretended to be asleep, and the boundaries between the reality and the illusion sometimes disappeared.

"What veal are we in," Egg asked as he woke with a start to the darkened outlines of heads rising above the bus seats in front. The washroom door flopped open and the back of the vehicle was suddenly lit with an ethereal aura of a flourescent blue glow. The stink was impossible. He struggled to open the window in front of him. It stuck and he hit it with his fist, repeatedly until it came loose. The night wind from the highway blew in on him like the waves of a cool ocean washing over his forehead: the southern summer wind of Dixie, the farmland wind of Double A. He felt his brow-sweat evaporating.

"I got slopped with blue juice all over my dockers," announced the man who had just stepped out of the latrine cubicle. "That blue juice... will it wash out?" he inquired of anyone who might listen.

"Were you standing or sitting," asked a voice out of the darkness further up the rows.

"Standing," responded the man from the water closet, as if he had just been asked a factual question such as what his name was or his batting average.

Egg asked his question again. "What veal are we in?" and his voice grew emphatic and stressed the word "veal".

"You dumb cluck," someone called out. "We didn't have veal for supper. We had chicken."

"Hey," said another anoynmous voice, "the Egg is clucking now. Like a hen," and there were some murmurs of laughter. The lights from passing trucks on the split interstate flashed in the young player's eyes. Egg, Hen, it made no difference.

"Ville, then, or however you say it," he responded half-heartedly to the taunt. The South was full of villes. Greensville. Knoxville. Clarksville. Fayetteville, Tennessee. Fayetteville, Georgia. Fayetteville, North Carolina. Heresville and Theresville. And every little ville had a Double A club. He could remember the spelling because ville had two ells, one for each A of the league. He just wanted to know where he was. There was such a darkness around him.

"Hey Hen, we're in Pallookasville." It didn't matter who had said that. He'd heard it before.

He would always be the last one on the bus. After his shower, he would sneak back to the field and watch as the keepers turned out the lights. The airy vastness of the bleachers in the old parks would open into an expanse of stars. The moon would shine down upon the box.

One night something inside him told him to point to the outfield fence. He stood at the plate, raised an index finger to the far wall and called the shot. He swung at an imaginary fastball on the O and two pitch. The Manager fined him for being late for the bus.

"Sometimes," he confided to yet another elderly couple who put him up in a room their own boy had vacated for a northern job, "sometimes the darkness creeps in around you and all you can do is think about heading toward the light. I'm going to the show real soon. I am. I am."

* * *

The rooms of the upper house had cooled in the night. That southern breeze had hung around all winter and followed him north, damp, almost sea-green in its sensation against the sweat-covered flesh of his back. Perhaps it was the spirit of his past three summers following him from Florida through the Carolina's, trailing him north to the "towns" of Triple A, and waiting for him to swallow his desire, his youth, his ambitions, its dark eyes peering at him from the shadows beneath the stands, from the dark and open mouths of the long tunnels that burrowed inward beneath the crowd, down into the bowels of hell itself where the groundskeepers played cards and chatted about forgotten names that even the record books had trouble remembering.

Or perhaps that hot breeze was the breath of the woman beside him, Dolores was her name, her heavy, methodical breathing a sign of life in the darkness. He reached down and pulled the sheet over his legs, and in the flood of purple light that seeped through the angel hair of the motionless sheer lace curtains ringed around the window with the solemnity of exhausted ghosts, the limbs of his body appeared to be the limbs of someone else, someone foreign, unknown, a stranger in his midst. They were the arms and legs of a man. The boy inside trembled. There was power there now.

* * *

"You're a proud little sonnuvabitch, ain't you," the reporter said after he had shut off the tape recorder.

"Whaddya mean?" asked the young man with a quizzical look on his face. "I only told you how I won the game. I won the game, and you saw it and the statistics will back me up. If you think that's being proud, then that's being proud. And if you think I'm such a proud little sonnuvabitch, as you put it, then go talk to some loser in the other dressing room who ain't so proud of what he's done tonight, and stop wasting my time." The player felt it was time to come out of his shell.

As the reporter made his way out through the throng of showered bodies, the player turned to the man with the next locker who had watched the whole incident and said nothing. "Whaddahe think I'm gunna say, anyways, with my dick hanging out in front of him and I'm butt naked except for my shower thongs?"

"You could have given a little credit to the guys on this club who scored the other four runs, the guys who pitched the shut-out tonight, the guys who sold the dogs and popcorn, the guys who took the tickets. You don't get it, do you? You live entirely in yourself. You don't talk to anyone on the bus. You just sit there, reading to yourself or staring off into some sleep-like trance with your hat pulled over your eyes. You don't let anyone know what you're so engrossed in. Planet earth to Hen. Calling Hen. Come in." The guy zipped up his fly, tucked in his shirt and walked away.

When Hen came back to the apartment that night Dolores was asleep. He opened the fridge for a moment and considered another beer, but thought better. He stood for a moment in the doorway of the room where he slept with her that season when the team was home. She had promised him her love, but all he had promised her was that he was going to the show, come hell, come high water. The window was open. The southern breeze was there again.

She turned and sat up in bed. "I've been waiting for you Honey Hen," she said. "Where've you been? Didn't you remember our dinner tonight?"

She reached out her arms and as she sat up, the thin white cotton summer sheet fell from her breasts and their large round nipples stared at him as if they had asked a question he couldn't answer. He lay naked beside her, her breath easing into his ears to remind him of who he was, where he had come from, and how mortal he could be when he wasn't on the field.

He thought he had wakened in the night and got up to go to the washroom, but the corridor of the tiny upstairs apartment seemed to roar in his ears. When he turned to look behind him there was that white light again, and in the other direction the darkness. He could go back or he could go ahead. The light seared and pained him to the centre of his soul when he looked at it. "Pallookasville, Pal," a voice whispered in his ear.

He woke suddenly, shaking, his body drenched in sweat, his fingers stiffened around an invisible bat, and Dolores holding him.

"Its all right honey Hen. Shh. Shh. Its all right."

A few weeks later, the team had just returned from a ten game road swing and were celebrating the fact that they were in first place. Hen sat out front in the batting title chase and was buying drinks for the boys and the women at the bar. He felt like the King of the World as the blond in the tight top hung from his flexed bicep. "I got other muscles too. Wanna see 'em?" The boys laughed. The music grew louder.

At four a.m. he crept up the stairs to the tiny apartment. Dolores was sitting in the living room with a dim single light throwing tantrums of shadows around the room. The floor was strewn with pieces of photographs people had taken of them together. Her cheeks were stained with tears and her eyes were red.

"Honey?" asked Hen, straightening himself and trying not to appear drunk.

Dolores simply pointed to a note on the coffee table. It bore the name of the parent club's General Manager and a phone number. "You've been called up. Leave and don't come back," she said.

* * *

"Remember! Remember!" the Manager shouted as the young player mounted the steps of the dugout. The crowd was cheering wildly. Rhythmic clapping broke out in the upper levels.

"Hey Chicken Man, remember what I told you!" shouted the Third Base Coach as the young batter warmed up in the on-deck circle, swinging his doughnutted bat above his head and feeling the muscles in his back and chest and shoulders stretch and pull beneath the weight and motion.

His name was announced: "Batting left, the second baseman, Bill Henholtz." Score tied, two on, two out, bottom of the eighth.

"Always remember who you are because you might not recognize who you become," the old guy he'd rented a room from in single A had told him in a moment of unsolicited fatherly advice. "Remember that," and the point had been punctuated with a raised finger. "Remember."

Signs were flashed by the Manager and the Coach as the player stepped into the box, wild signs, a frenzied semaphore. The runner at second nodded.

The runner at first nodded toward the plate. It was like someone was speaking to him in language for the deaf, spelling out each letter. "R-E-M-E-M-B-E-R" followed by what he could have sworn was the signal for slide. He squinted, but his eyes just wouldn't register.

"Remember!" all the fans seemed to shout from the upper decks. The organist played DUMP-DUMP-DUMP, over and over until the stadium shook with excitement. The scoreboard in left field glowed with his egg-like statistics. He stepped up to the plate.

He looked down at the Catcher who spit through the grill work of his mask. "Gunna remember?" he thought the Catcher asked.

He looked toward the Third Base Coach who had stopped transmitting the plays from the bench and had folded his arms in a gesture of sublime contentment. He nodded yes, but what the player wanted was assurance. Clarification.

The Base Coach figured the batter had the situation in-hand and nodded back.

The guy selling the hot dogs to the people in the expensive seats nodded.

The guys in the bullpen who peered anxiously through the outfield fence nodded in unison.

Some jerk who'd taken off his shirt and painted his body in team colours, sat high up near the first base foul pole where no one can really see or be seen and nodded.

Down the first base line, a little girl in a team cap too big for her head nodded because everyone else was doing it.

A warm wind eased over the stands from the south end of the stadium. It wrapped itself around his neck like an old lover who had come to plead for another night.

"This is it," he said to himself. "Now just remember..." He steadied the bat over his shoulder for the swing, its tip rotated in a gently threatening motion. His neck sank into his shoulders. "Shit, though. Remember what?"

And suddenly he remembered. He was in a narrow corridor with a bright light at one end. As he stood there with a muffled roaring all around him, he knew that if he walked toward the light a great wounding pain would open inside him. If he pressed toward the darkness he would waken away from the pain of constant trying, constant striving, the anxiety others would call accomplishment but that he would only feel to be something eating away at him from inside. The moment he had waited for all his life was upon him.

The player turned to the Ump and asked for time. The Ump shook his head. "Play ball." The words seemed to echo through the batter's head; soundless sounds down a long corridor.

The pitcher was about to go into his wind-up. He drew his shoulders up, pulled the ball to his chest, and suddenly relaxed his arms again and spread his stance. Something was weird at the plate.

The bat had slipped from the batters fingers and fallen to the ground, and his hands had turned palms up in a pleading gesture at the Umpire. "I'm sorry, but I can't remember," the batter said as he turned and nodded politely to the Ump and the Catcher. He looked about madly for a solution and backed out of the batter's box.

"Time" bellowed the official in frustration. Flies hovered in tiny constellations, illuminated by the late afternoon sunlight that shone upon the mound.

The Manager sprang from the dugout. "What the hell's wrong with you, Henholtz? Don't you remember?" The Manager was right up in his face.

The player could see the Manager's eyes bulging into his, the tiny little red lines that almost seemed to throb with the question, beating and beating. "Henholtz! Henholtz! Get that look outta your eye and pay attention to me! You having a stroke or a conniption or something?" the Manager screamed. "Well? Say something!"

The player looked into the Manager's angry eyes with a calm, distant expression as if he had just gazed through the portals of paradise. In a low, slow, almost inaudible voice the player began to speak. "When to the sessions of sweet silent thought I summon up remembrance of things past."

"Henholtz! Don't you quote Byron to me at a time like this! We're tied, two men on, two out with the bloody pennant on the line."

The young player blinked incomprehensibly, shook his head and turned toward the dugout. The entire stadium watched in murmured confusion as the player's back, name and number, disappeared down the dark corridor.

Perhaps he paused there, but for how long no one can be sure. From the field and the stands, the corridor was a long, dark, gaping maw that had swallowed players, old and young, who had come up the long, hard way, only to find their exit.

A great silence filled the stadium. The Manager dipped into his bench and gave another man the chance that destiny had set aside for Bill Henholtz.

* * *

The wind had come up from the south and was blowing fly balls off their course that summer night so long ago. "Remember how they'll drift on you," the Coach had said as he patted him on the head and the teams of youngsters changed for another inning. "Remember now."

A late, dusky sun was just disappearing over the tree tops, and the boy squinted into the space above the batter's head. He inched left from second to cover the gap toward first, allowing the runner to lead off if he wanted, and hoping the batter would hit into a double play.

Rain had fallen just before supper that evening, and the ground all through the game had glistened like a great green emerald carpet. The batter stepped up to the box, stopping momentarily to adjust a helmet that was too big for him.

The second baseman stared at the man on first, and then glanced over at his coach who stood with the other kids in the little concrete dugout where he had scrawled his name and message to posterity in an inconspicuous spot the day before: *Billy Henholtz played here on his way to the Majors.*

The pitch came, the ball popped up, arching in a high, fluid curve before the life suddenly left it. In that instant he looked into the setting sun. The light that filled his eyes stung deeply into his brain with an enormous, flashing pain. His eyes shut automatically. He couldn't remember where the ball would be. "Long way up, short way down," yelled his Coach. The other kids were screaming. Even a blind man could have seen it.

On the way home the boy sat silently in the car. The window was rolled down and the soft night breeze blew across his forehead and blissed his sweat. He closed his eyes and saw the baseball player again at the edge of the tunnel and held out a ball for an autograph.

"Not today kid," said the player, "its been rough out there." The boy looked puzzled. "Just remember kid," said the player, "you always live with your failures. Deep down inside, they never really go away."

And as the daydream player turned away from the boy and disappeared down the long darkness of the tunnel, the boy read the name on the player's back: HENHOLTZ.

"Little league is just a game, dear," his Mother said in an attempt to sooth his wound, her eyes fixed not on her son but on the on-coming traffic of the rural highway that sped toward them like stars shot down a long tunnel. The lights of passing cars kept blinking on and off on her face so that all her features disappeared into the night and out of the reach of memory. "You can go back tomorrow and it will be a whole new ball game."

"Can I really?" he said with a heavy note of raw skepticism in his voice that his Mother had never heard before. "Can I really?"

Sunlight Park

i) Cannonball

Ned "Cannonball" Crane was the greatest player ever to wear the uniform of a Toronto ball club. He isn't remembered on a plaque at Cooperstown or even a marker in Toronto. You can ask for him at the Skydome, but they won't have heard of him. The oldtimers, whose memories reach back before the days of Hanlan's Point and Maple Leaf Stadium, will shake their heads when they are asked about the man named for his amazing arm who almost single-handedly won the city's first professional sports championship. He remains a shadow. The park, Sunlight Park, where he won his laurels is far beyond memory now, buried beneath the layers of lives that have built and rebuilt the city. The Lords of Baseball who sit in judgement on the game have let his story slip into the black oblivion of time and death, so that to search for Cannonball is like looking for sunlight in the darkest moment of your days; for the manner of his death has obscured the triumphs of his life.

According to Frank E. Butler, a contemporary of Crane's who wrote "Ned Crane -- The Great Long Distance Thrower," Cannonball earned his nickname at the age of seventeen when he won a throwing contest in Worcester, Massachusetts in 1879. The distance, as far as Butler remembered it, was three hundred and fifty-one feet. Butler says Crane threw "a ball on Boston Common four hundred and seventeen feet, but I don't know who measured the throw and Crane was never interested himself about it as he never thought it would be recorded." Just for the sake of comparison, the deepest alley in the majors is Death Valley in centre at Tiger Stadium. That measures four hundred and forty feet. Butler continues: "While Crane's longest throw has not been authenticated, it has been established that he has made more and longer throws than any man living. There are many living today who were present when he made a series of phenomenal throws at the old Union Grounds in Boston...the longest throws ever made by a ball player. The throws were never officially measured, however, and therefore never went on record -- and, so it seems, was the case with all Crane's exhibition throws."

In St. Louis in 1884, the owner of the local team bet the young prodigy that he couldn't throw a ball more than four hundred and ten feet. Crane, never afraid of a good dare, took the bet against his teammates' advice. Fifty dollars was put on the line. Crane blew a ligament in his arm while trying. The throw was a yard short.

When Crane signed the largest minor league contract to date to play for the Torontos of the fledgling International League, the hackles were raised in the Toronto press. Twenty-eight hundred dollars a year was the League's top salary; Crane doubled that. The Toronto owners, however, gambled that Crane might be worth the money.

New rules came into the game that season. The mound was moved fifteen feet closer to home. No longer could a pitch be delivered underhand. The era of power hurling had entered the game. Crane let it be known that he had mastered the new methods.

Throughout the season Crane was in and out of the line-up. Injuries were seldom reported then. Wild pitches were recorded, and Crane had plenty. On May 19, Crane was battered by the Rochester squad, 11-5, and *The Globe* lit into the pitcher with venom: "To begin with, Crane the pitcher was erratic and was only saved by Traffley [the catcher and idol of the fans from the previous season] from making many serious misplays at critical moments. He was battered hard and did not sustain the character expected from the highest paid man in the International League." What made matters worse was that the game was a sell-out with an overflow crowd of 4,500, many of whom stood watching in the outfield. The Governor General, Lord Landsdowne, was in attendance. The long, hot summer of 1887 had just begun.

But gradually, the Toronto club began to climb the standings. By September 17, with two games remaining in the schedule against the first place outfit from Newark, Toronto stood only a game out of first. A victory would tie them with Newark; two wins would give Toronto the grail.

The early morning of September 17, 1887 was foggy. The field was an eerie, almost ethereal dreamscape. The wooden bleachers faded in and out of the white mist. A silence hung still and breathless like a dragon waiting to devour a knight errant. But as the fog lifted, the crowds came. They stood fifteen deep in places. Ten thousand. They piled into the stands, they crowded the foul areas and the outfield. The police pushed them back to clear the area of play, but even the constables fell in among the packed observers as the teams took the field and the sun burned a watchful eye through the opaque late summer sky.

By noon the fog was just a memory and Toronto had its tie in hand. Crane was the pitcher of decision, 15-5, over the vaunted Jersey squad. The clubs broke for lunch. Few spectators gave up their seats. The air smelled of baked potatoes and cigar smoke and beer.

The city waited for the final game to decide the champion. The big question was who would pitch the deciding game. Crane was Toronto's best, but in order to make the last game meaningful, the homeside had gambled everything on Crane's morning performance. After him the rotation was weak. Would Crane throw the second game? Impossible. No arm could last that long. The prospects for a win seemed bleak.

The Globe reports what happened next: "As soon as it was made clear that Crane was to pitch the second game, hundreds leaped to their feet and cheered frantically, a mighty whirl of enthusiasm took everybody within its embrace, and an astounding volume of sound shook the stands and swept down toward the city and out over the grounds like the march of a tornado."

CRANE! CRANE! CRANE!

Through the first three innings Cannonball was perfect. But at the top of the fourth, he walked the lead-off man. When a routine infield roller started to move the runners, Crane scooped up the ball and tried to run it to second for the out. As he crossed the bag he seemed to lose his balance and spun out in a cloud of dust.

Pain paralysed his face. He clutched at his ankle. The Manager ran on the field, the umpires gathered round. He had sprained his right. His push-off leg. Visibly in pain, Crane staggered back to the mound and walked the next batter, then threw wild on a third strike. The runners went.

Traffley fought his way through the crowd who lined the foul zone directly behind the plate. Where was the ball? The sphere careened off a forest of pantlegs, deeper and deeper into the assembled. An eager fan picked it up and held it aloft as a trophy.

The catcher grabbed at the ball, knocking the on-looker sprawling, turned and flung himself like a wild beast toward the plate; but the slide came too late. The runners scored. Newark 4 Toronto 0.

Crane doubled over on the mound. Only one out. The inning looked like a rout. But he dug down deep. There was magic in his arm. He threw the ball harder and faster than he had ever thrown it before. The Newark side sat down.

By the bottom of the eighth, Crane was still in the game. It was his turn to bat. The score was 4-1, bases loaded. Crane hit a double. The game was tied. The park went wild. The crowd could be heard across the Don as far as Sherborne and the Allen Gardens. And through the ninth and the tenth the two sides struggled, each fighting to survive. Winner take all. The game remained a saw-off.

By the eleventh, Crane had again shut down the Newark order. He had just pitched his twentieth inning of the day. His ankle was so swollen he had to limp from the dugout to the plate with the aid of two bats as crutches. The grounds fell silent.

The first pitch came. Low and outside. Crane watched it go by. He paused for a moment and winced. He glanced up at the sky as if he was searching for a miracle. The sunlight bit into his eyes.

The second pitch. He swung, and for an instant there was an explosion deep inside him, a fierce shout welling up from his soul and a bang in his hands that screamed both pain and joy through every electrified sinew of his body. The ball left the bat. It rose. It rose over the infield and outfield, high over the heads of the throng deep to centre. It sailed into the sun and was eaten by its flames.

The following Monday morning, September 19, 1887,

Torontonians opened their newspapers and relived the moment: *"And then the mighty audience arose and cheered and stamped and whistled and smashed hats..the frantic fans dashed onto the field and carried Crane aloft as his foot touched home."* This was victory. Argonauts, Maple Leafs, Blue Jays would add their names to the roll. But this day was the first.

Crane left Toronto in 1888. News of his shining moment had spread to the National League where he was signed by Mike "King" Kelly to play for the New York Giants. He arrived in New York, but the magic got left behind.

He went 5-6 on the season against heavy hitting, still managing a 2.43 ERA. And even though he had a losing record, Albert Goodwill Spalding, magnate of the great game, thought enough of Cannonball to add him to the World Tour Team in 1888.

Crane pitched his way across the States, the South Seas and Europe for John Montgomery Ward's All American Squad, and much to Spalding's surprise, managed to score several wins against the immortal White Stockings of 1888.

In a moment of triumph, the two touring teams stopped in Egypt where they played a game at the base of the Pyramids and posed for a souvenir photograph on the paws and shoulders of the inscrutable Sphinx. And there, standing proudly atop the creature's shoulders is Ned "Cannonball" Crane.

By 1894, his career was history. Two years later, and almost nine years to the day of the famous game at the Baseball Grounds on Queen Street East, the city of Toronto was seen from the American shore as a mirage hovering above Lake Ontario. Fluke weather. A trick of nature. But there it was.

The next day, Crane, exhausted from searching for a way back to the game he loved, his arm blown out and his hopes dashed, was found dead in a room of a Rochester hotel. And the legend died with him.

ii) David

But the story doesn't end there. In fact, it is where mine begins. It is where Crane's story, by surrogate, becomes the one I am still trying to tell myself. The truth is a hard thing to find; sometimes it just can't be reached. I pursued the story of one fated hero because I wanted to understand another.

Maybe Crane just got in the way. A handy, accidental obsession. The therapists say I have made a mask for grief. But to me the search for Cannonball offered an avenue to understanding, a way out, an intercessor.

Grief entered my life one winter night. My wife and I were reading in bed, some big band music playing softly from the nightstand radio. We were waiting for our son to come home from a party. Someone was singing Jerome Kern's "All the Things You Are."

The doorbell rang. The police had come to tell us that our son David had been in an accident. *Under the influence. Alcohol and some other substance. No one else hurt. Prognosis is poor and even if there is recovery his brain... He survived the crash but not the overdose.*

Overdose. A chaplain's hand at the hospital. My wife's head on my shoulder. I can feel her body heaving and shaking against mine. The walls were so white. So final. So final...

I wished the numbness would leave our lives. My soul turned white. It froze everything. My senses, my thoughts.

I would watch my wife as she stared from the windows of our home, and there was nothing I could say, no way across the distance to melt the glacier of pain that moved between us so gradually. She was in her suffering and I was in mine.

The first anniversary of David's death was almost on us. There had been no summer that year. Just white time where there should have been life.

In sleep I had been grinding my teeth, trying to make sense of what had happened to the three of us, my wife, my son and me. I had ground the tops off my molars and cracked some of my incisors. I ended up sitting in the dentist's office, waiting to have my mouth reconstructed.

I took a copy of a baseball magazine called *Dugout* from the stack of waiting room reading. Baseball was what we did together, David and I. I thought it brought us closer. I thought it made us more father and son.

Goodbye Mr. Spalding

As I read, it was just like we were together again. Father and son. He would watch some amazing play with a glorious look of awe on his face, and then turn to me and ask "did you see that?" Or when Molitor or Carter crossed the plate, David would stand up and scream "Yes!" at the top of his lungs.

My Grandfather had taken me to Maple Leaf Stadium before they tore it down, and he had regaled me with legends of Hanlan's Point and Ruth's first homerun on the eve of the Great World War. My father and I had been at the Ex for the Jay's first game when Doug Ault homered against the White Sox to set the divine machine in motion once again. David and I were there on October 23, 1993, when Joe Carter's blast made time stand still. I saw the lineage stretching through me and David far into the future.

When I took David to the Jays games, we liked to sit high up in the 500 level where the blue sky and the bright sun are as close as you can get to heaven on a July afternoon in Toronto, and the field unfolds before you like a map of the world. The 500 level is for dreamers and optimists. I thought David and I shared the same dream.

I tried to turn David into my hero. I imagined him playing college ball, getting spotted by a big league scout. A father and son interview on TSN.

And watching him playing his first major league game on the field at Skydome, I'd think "there's a little piece of me out there." I'd look at him and I'd feel like I'd live forever.

When David died my dreams died too.

What is even harder to understand is how he could have thrown it all away like that. I thought he had it in him. The grit. The strength.

When he was eleven and on a little league team in the north end, there was this game to decide first place in his division, and it mattered. It really meant everything to the season. David dove for a catch in the outfield. Made a beautiful play of it. But he rolled on the ground and didn't get up. I ran onto the field with the coaches.

He'd dislocated his shoulder. The pain must have been intense. And all the time I was driving him to the hospital and telling him what a great catch he'd made, he kept saying he had to get back, and trying to imagine what inning they were in. I really felt for him when the doctor said he couldn't catch a ball for three months. "Yeah," I said, "but that last one will leave'em talking."

As I read the magazine article "Toronto's Fields of Yesteryear," all my memories came flooding back. They were the first real, warm living thing I'd been able to feel for ages. The crowd. The players. The summer days. But one name jumped off the page and hit me like a lightning bolt between the eyes: Sunlight Park. Where the legacy began.

Great name for a ball park. All the images of summer, innocence, childhood joy, cool green grass and timelessness. As I imagined it, I could almost smell the cigar smoke, the baked potatoes -- because this was before pop corn and hot dogs -- the creaking wooden stands, the summer. I imagined the grass shimmering in the morning dew just before the start of a daylight double-header. It seemed so perfect; it seemed so baseball.

In reality, Sunlight Park took its name from Lever Brothers 'Sunlight Soap.' The soap-works were just beyond the outfield fence. The park stood on an oblong parcel of land which straddled the banks of the slow, dirty and brown Don River. In its heyday, it lay outside the boundaries of the City of Toronto, almost the other side of Jordan.

In the old *Goad's Atlas* of 1890 in the Metro Reference Library, a book of district by district maps that were drawn for calculating fire insurance, is the only depiction of Sunlight Park -- an aerial representation of the tiny wooden grandstand. The outfield is subdivided into narrow parcels of land. Even in its time, no one thought the place would be around for long. No one even bothered to take a picture. The entire citizenry approached the new phenomenon of a professional sports field tenuously -- they wanted to see whether the fad would last before they made any commitment to it, and by the time it caught on, the sun had set on Sunlight Park and it was no more.

Today the area is covered by the on-ramp for the Don Valley Parkway, a Toyota dealership, a factory, some old houses, and the parking lot for Lever Brothers. A tiny street that led to the park, an avenue of gothic-roofed workers cottages known as Baseball Place, has disappeared beneath the layers of progress. Somewhere, just paces behind the cluster of bright new Tercels, is the centre of a forgotten summer universe: the site of home plate.

And right below the brief mention of the park in that magazine article I saw the words "and the first major star for the Toronto club was a pitcher named Ned 'Cannonball' Crane." That was how I discovered Crane.

I've always had a thing for baseball nicknames. Zeke Banana Nose Bonura. Ding-a-Ling Clay. Bunions Zeider. But of all the nicknames, Cannonball, for a pitcher, carries the implication of greatness. Cannonball. Someone who could deliver. Like the jazz great Cannonball Adderley. Power. Force. The hardball.

With my mouth still numb from the dental anaesthesia, I went home and dashed off a letter to the Baseball Hall of Fame in Cooperstown, and several weeks later came the reply.

In the packet were several xeroxes. There was his pitching record from *The Baseball Registry* which charted a mediocre career from its rise to its decline, with the sad inevitability that follows even the greats up one side of the mountain and down the other.

Another xeroxed article contained a photograph of a handsome young man with neatly combed hair and a moustache. It was written around the turn of the century by a fellow player named Frank Butler and detailed Crane's exploits as a champion thrower. I saw Jesse Barfield at the peak of his career in right field for the Jays make a throw like the one Butler described; a bullet; no cut-off man; just pure, clean power and speed; an arm like a gun; a ball like a shot out of a cannon.

And finally, at the back of the gathering of sheets, was the obituary from *Sporting Life*, September 26, 1896. He'd died young. Tragically. It spoke of Crane's throwing exploits, briefly mentioned his career, the fact that he'd had a stint with Spalding's 1888 World Tour Team, and that his latter career had been plagued by drinking:

NED CRANE IS DEAD.
Sad Ending Of A Once Great
Ball Player.
The Unfortunate Man Dies Among

Bruce Meyer

*Strangers and Alone From the
Effects of an Overdose of Chloral
Accidentally Taken.*

Overdose. I could see the word in bold type hung like a black cloud over his head. *Overdose.* The ugly suspicion of suicide. Between the lines I saw the Lords of Baseball frowning upon Crane, shucking away his life, his career, his memory because he had died alone with no one to answer his call for help. No one listening.

Heroes, saieth the Lords of Baseball, do not die of an overdose.

I had wanted to believe that David did not die of an overdose. I still cannot believe that word. It is a word that comes in a manilla envelope from the Coroner's Office. It is a word that I detest.

I know the way the Lords of Baseball think. I know they will never pardon Shoeless Joe; they will never forgive Pete Rose's gambling; and I know they will never acknowledge Cannonball Crane.

Here was a story that needed to be told, an explanation pleading to be offered. A life that had been submerged by the way he had died.

Overdose.

There had to be a reason. There had to be some vindication. Here was a hero: why should he be tarnished? If Crane was good enough to be chosen by Alfred Spalding to play with the best of the game in 1888, then there had to be a reason, a legend in his own time that demanded to be repeated. I made up my mind to tell that story, a story which was hidden beneath the layers of lost seasons.

I phoned Rochester for the Coroner's report and was put on hold for twenty minutes by an overworked clerk who couldn't comprehend my reasons for wanting what I wanted. "Wouldn't a death certificate do?"

I wrote to the Canadian Medical Association. *"Dear Sirs: I am currently doing some research on a nineteenth century baseball star who died of "an accidental dose of Chloral." Could you please tell me what this substance is, what its effects are, etc. Did people take Chloral to commit suicide?"*

A polite response which had been forwarded to a medical historian at the University of Toronto informed me that in the nineteenth century chloralhydrate was a widely prescribed though addictive somnolent. If taken in sequential doses it would produce a good sleep the first night and a state of depression the next day, which would, in turn, cause the patient to take a larger dose the next night and have an even larger hangover and feeling of depression the next day. Taken with alcohol, chloralhydrate could be fatal. Had the individual in question consumed any alcohol before taking the remedy? Taken in larger doses, chloralhydrate would shut down the body's nervous system and produce death. It was not prescribed after 1932.

So, what if Crane had not intended to kill himself? There was no note. The last person to see him alive said he was depressed. But what if the depression was a result of the chloral? Perhaps all he wanted was a good night's sleep.

The Lords of Baseball take note. I intend to file an appeal.

Every day, my daydreams were filled with Cannonball Crane, and I grew more and more obsessed. For the first time in over a year, I had something other than my own grief to consider and I latched onto it like a life-raft.

I pictured Crane rifling balls around Boston Common. I imagined him being welcomed to Toronto. I envisioned his struggle in front of the Governor-General during a bad game and my heart went out to him.

I was winding through back issues of *Sporting Life* on a microfilm machine in the basement of the Metro Reference Library. Images of lost lives and forgotten days whirred past and became a blur. "September 1887." I slowed the reels.

The etching of a ball player. Handle-bar moustache. There was Crane. A young man. Life glows in his face. The whole world is there in front of him. This guy can pitch. The archetypal hero.

I imagine I am standing on first base at Sunlight Park. He is pitching cannonballs over an empty home plate. He reaches way back and digs deeply into his wind-up. Lightning flashes over the city. He unleashes a meteor -- a bullet of ice and rock flung as if it is shot from the farthest edge of the universe. And as quickly as it leaves his fingers, the ball vanishes into eternity.

He stands upright again, looks down the pike and straightens his jersey. He turns to me and nods.

Me: Are You Crane? Ned "Cannonball" Crane?

Crane: Yep

Me: Wow. I mean, I've been reading about you. I've been trying to research your life and explain your...your death. I hope you don't mind me mentioning that.

Crane: I suppose not. It happened. There's no denying that. What do you want to know?

Me: What happened on Spalding's World Tour? That seems to have been your high water mark.

Crane: I had a good time. I had a real good time. [He looks down at the ground. He can tell what I'm thinking.] I...I discovered the party life. "Champagne Charlie" as the old song goes? I'd leave the field with hell going on in my shoulder. A drink here, a sip there, and I'd feel better. It made me feel like my arm wasn't going to come off. It made me feel like I'd live forever and that my career would last that long too.

Me: I see.

Crane: Why don't we get down to why you're really here?

Me: I'm here to find out the truth about a forgotten hero who took a bum rap.

Crane: You really want to know about David, but somehow I just got in the way and for a time my story took your mind off that ache that's been burning away deep down inside of you.

Me: So?

Crane: You need to close a door on that part of your life and get on with what you have to do. Because there aren't any reasons. Because you can't explain why certain things happen.

That night in Rochester, you know what I was thinking? I was thinking how good it would be to get home and see my wife and kid, and how a night's sleep would set me right on the road in the morning. That's why there wasn't any note. I'd seen the vision of Toronto when it was hovering there, and in the back of my mind, I thought maybe they'll need someone next year to work with the team and maybe I can get back there because that mirage was a sign. And then, well, surprise!

And you've got questions. Questions are for the living. There's a point where a person gets beyond them, but as long as you're alive, you ask things of yourself. But there aren't always answers. Like in mathematics. You live with the axioms; things you can't prove; you just accept them and get on with what you're doing.

Me: I don't know if I have the courage. It's a big leap.

Crane: Afraid of the answers?

Me: Possibly.

Crane: Axioms. *(Pause)*. What was he like?

Me: David? *(Crane nods)*. I have trouble remembering. Honest. He seems to grow more distant every day. It's like an old photograph someone has left in the light too long.

Crane: Try. *(Pause)*.

Me: Hey, what was it like to stand on top of the Sphinx?

Crane: Like a happy ending. Good answers are like happy endings; there just aren't always enough to go around. Hey, yeah, it would have been great just to stop the story there when I was on top of the world, but things don't work that way. People make their own stories out of their lives, and when someone else wants to repeat them the tales can't always be told the way we'd like to tell them. And when we can't live with the truth we seek to invent something else. I wish I could help you. I really do. But that's the way it is.

No matter how often I replay it in my mind, the interview always ends in the same way. All I have is the facts. They aren't much. They are only jottings on paper. I wish they would let me lie.

iii) There

Even though we are in the middle of an empty parking lot in a rough area of the city, my wife is patient as I search for Cannonball Crane. The sun sets on a perfect summer evening, the sky greens above us and the warmth passes from its light.

Behind us where the foul line once demarcated the boundaries between dreams and reality, the city's buildings stand at attention like a starting line-up during the national anthems. A row of poplars wavers gently in the cool, dusky breeze as if they were flags along an outfield fence. My wife sidles up to me and takes my hand.

"This is where it all began," I say softly to her. "This is Sunlight Park." I know at that moment what an anthropologist must feel if unearths something older than Leakey found in the dust of aeons.

"Look," I say and point north toward the dealership and the warehouse that sprawl along Queen. A street car rumbles in the distance. "That's where the stands were."

I want her to see this as I have come to see it, not as a place where nothing exists, but as a place where possiblities remain, the home of all the once-upon-a-times that live in the centre of our imaginations.

And I can see old Sunlight Park as I start to describe it to her. For about two hundred feet, the covered bleachers rise out of the soil of my city and face south toward the soap works, the old distillery and the lake. I pace off the distance.

"We're in the outfield now," I say to her, my voice falling to a whisper as if we are in a church. "Cannonball Crane is at the plate. The area behind us is filled with fans who lined up at Nordheimer's Piano works on Yonge Street to buy shin-plaster tickets."

"How much is a shin-plaster, again?"

"Twenty-five cents, paper money. The fans who arrive late find the stands are filled, but they don't mind because they're here and they're part of the day. The homeside is down by several runs, but they have men on the bases.

Traffley the catcher is measuring his strides from first and inching his way toward second and keeping his eye on the pitcher. Slattery, the Toronto left-fielder is tagging at second. He's concentrating on the pitch, watching the pitcher's fingers as the ball tumbles in his glove like the mechanism of a combination safe. Cannonball is at bat. He braces his feet and stares at the gunner as if he's looking into eternity. And he is... The entire stadium is holding its breath.

Suddenly, there's the pitch. You can hear it crack off the bat. It rises, higher and higher into the air, and like everyone here you can feel the triumph, the thrill of the moment rise up in your throat because you know, you just know where that ball is going.

The Newark outfielder races farther and farther back. His footsteps are thundering closer and closer and you almost think he's going to run you down and everyone around you pushes tighter and tighter to make way for this charging gladiator. But the ball soars over his head and drops behind the feet of the fielder who turns and picks it up and hurls it to second as the limping Crane arrives on his stand-up double.

The stadium goes wild. They can smell the victory. The game is tied. The momentum is now with Toronto. But it isn't over yet.

All they have to do is cash in. Two innings go by. Crane is still at pitching, still shutting down Newark. He's exhausted, he's hurt, and the pressure is on him to win the game. The first pitch. "Strike!" hollers the Umpire.

The next pitch is in the glove. The pitcher examines the ball as if it's the solution to a question of life or death. He stares at Crane who is flexing his bat, feeling for the strike zone. The pitch comes. Hard. Fast. Crane swings. And suddenly, like a spark in the night, the ball catches fire. It rises and rises. The Newark fielder runs back, back. He tramples into the crowd who catch him. But that ball is high. It's gone. The game is history.

And Crane? He begins his limping victory march round the bases. Every step is a joyous struggle. There are hats in the air. Fans flood onto the field. His teammates run to meet him. And alone, all alone, as the crowd presses closer and closer to be the first to touch him when the deed is done, Crane staggers forward and touches home plate. Toronto has won the title. Like Carter's shot in the '93 Series. It happens here, only this time there is nothing to compare it to. This is the first time the city has tasted victory."

My wife squeezes my hand. "Let's get some supper," she says, and I agree because the game is over and the ghosts of September 1887 have long gone home.

We are sitting in a pleasant restaurant by the harbour. The boats pass up and down, and in the twilight their running lights reflect with a yellow summer moon off the green-black waters of the bay.

And then I realize what Cannonball was trying to tell me, what I have been trying to discover by finding Cannonball. Beneath all the questions there is David. David's life. His loves. His enthusiasms. I cannot forget them. They are the joy that even grief cannot destroy. The story unmasked at last.

I picture my boy. He is six years old. We are together in our backyard on a summer night like this. He makes his first catch.

I picture him playing T-Ball as an eight-year-old, running the bases with passion and fury and leaping for joy when he was driven home from third.

And there is David jumping to his feet and shouting "Mom! Mom!" and waving madly when the camera put us up on the Jumbotron in the Dome -- a million to one chance. There we are. And for every memory there is a moment of celebration, moments which now seem like so many lucky longshots.

David, my hero, my lost future. If we are measured by the heroes we choose, why were mine so fated? Why have I let the manner of their deaths overshadow the miracle of their lives? The only one forcing me to sit in judgement is myself. And now I realize what right have I? Do I trust the Lords of Baseball ahead of my own heart?

A few hours later, our summer evening is coming to an end. I have not seen my wife this relaxed in ages. We have needed this moment for a long long time. A little light in our lives.

I head back east along King Street rather than turn north toward our home. "Where are you going?" my wife asks.

"Back to Sunlight Park."

"Did you lose something there?"

"No," I reply. "I need another look."

"But it's dark now. How will you see?"

Something inside me is incomplete. "I just need one last look," I repeat, pleading with my wife for her indulgence of my whim. "On the way home."

We pull into the empty parking lot. Only the shadows of the soap works and the old factories remain now. Lights flicker like paired fireflies on the Parkway, and the stars are arguing with the city's glow for their rightful place in the sky. And at that moment it begins again.

There is bright sunlight and dewy grass sparkling as if this was the beginning of all time: a cool, fresh start. Two players are having a game of catch in the infield, and as I watch them a great empty and aching space is suddenly sealed in my heart.

A man in a cream-coloured old style cap and knickerbocker pants is throwing the ball to a teenage boy.

"That's it," says the man. "Keep it up. Put your shoulder into it."

I recognize the older of the two. He is wearing a handle-bar moustache. He sees me and nods in acknowledgement.

The other is harder to know. He is the one who follows me everywhere, in my sleep, my waking moments. He is the one I cannot let go, the ghost of a boy who is really no more than a child. His hair is blond and resting on his shoulders. His back is turned to me.

As the vision fades I know I have seen something in the darkness of a summer night that cannot completely be fathomed or understood; and they continue, their rhythm quickens, and they are almost one, absorbed and resolute in their game of catch.

They are getting on with their deaths.

I must get on with my life. I have the courage, now, to accept the fact that I never will have the answers to the questions of my son's death. And with that realization time begins again. Spring. Summer. The thaw has come.

"Yes," I tell my wife as I start the engine and close the car door. "There was light enough to see."

The Glove

Prologue)

Barney's Roadhouse has something extra to offer its patrons. Among the signed DiMaggio bats and the autographed Mantle jerseys, above the glass case and the chintzy saloon league cups topped by aspiring angels or tiny gilded batters, there hangs an ancient souvenir. It is a nostalgic talisman for local teams who come to toast its powers; and as luck would have it, Barney's came by it. You can touch it. It won't bite. Believe in it if you want. Try it on. Someone may even tell you its story.

i)

"There's Cap Anson rounding first and Bid McPhee coming in to score with the go-ahead run, followed by Amos Rusie!" the boy's Grandfather hollered in make-believe play-by-play as the child ran madly around the yard.

The point, so the runner believed, was to celebrate the bat's contact with the ball and touch as many bases as could be touched while the old man, doubled over with a stitch, rooted in the shrubs for the ball. Every tree, every bush, was a hot corner.

In the boy's imagination the garden was a splendid stadium, lush with emerald grass, and every leaf was the face of a fan, shouting with adoration. And the moment of supreme joy: his foot touched home plate, a bald patch in the garden grass where the grubs had eaten through.

So when the boy showed up at the tryouts, knowing that because he was six he was now eligible for the junior Church team, he was able to answer the Coach's question: "Have you ever played baseball?"

"Yes," said the boy, in the honest belief that he had.

"Then take the outfield," the Coach commanded and waved his arm in a widening arc that pointed the way to the schoolyard fence.

A soft morning breeze was blowing on his neck. The child felt very alone, very far away from the others as he stood there with sun beaming down on his forehead.

The Coach began practice by standing at the plate and shagging grounders to the infield. It soon got boring out there. The boy sat down on the spot.

"You there, outfield," cried the Coach, "get your ass outta the turf and play ball!" He pointed directly at the boy. "This one's for you, kiddo." The ball cracked off the bat and rose high into the brilliant sun. The boy followed it with his eyes and stared directly into the glare. It disappeared into a hundred little blue spheres that juggled and bounced in all directions.

The boy ran forward. His arms outstretched as if anticipating a hug, a kiss or a pick-me-up and spin. Half-blind, blinking and squinting, the ball landed at his feet and rolled between his legs. "Moron!" someone yelled. He ran to fetch the ball.

"Here's another," yelled the Coach with the crack of the bat. Again the sun was blinding, but this time as he faced the fly and his legs pumped him faster and faster toward the ball his feet took off beneath him and he landed face first on the ground. An old familiar tooth made a journey across his tongue. His instinct was to cry, but instead he spit it in his hand.

By the time he looked up, the team had gathered round. The Coach stood above him, glaring.

"It came out," said the boy with an air of surprise and held up the tooth as if anticipating an explanation.

"I thought you told me you played baseball! And where's your glove? Don't you have a glove?" The Coach stared sternly down upon him.

The boy fought back tears and shook his head.

"Geez," said the Coach, looking to heavens in desperation. "I can't be responsible if you break your fingers."

"Where do I get one?" came the plaintive question. A low, communal groan went up among the team, and laughter gradually crept through the ranks.

"Kid," said the Coach, "you'd better go home. Don't come back 'til you learn a lot more. Don't come back until you know ball." He turned to the others and hollered "let's hustle, men!" and the team scattered knowingly about the field.

The boy took his tooth and his wounded pride and watched for a while through the schoolyard fence before shuffling home like a newsreel soldier who had just surrendered to the enemy.

"How did it go?" his Mother asked. He didn't tell her he thought baseball sucked.

"I need a glove."

"Gloves are expensive. We can't afford one. Besides, when I spoke to the Reverend after church last week, he told me the parish would supply all you need. Now go wash your hands and get ready for lunch."

As he stood at the sink and washed his hands, he tried to imagine how a glove would feel. And when his parents checked for the tooth that night, he had not put it beneath his pillow.

ii)

His Grandfather had peered through the fence at Sunlight Park; he saw Ruth's first home run at Hanlan's Point; and through countless summers at the Maple Leaf grounds, he witnessed the rise and fall of every young comer, and wept when the wrecker's ball levelled the field. And now, the old man believed, he would sow the seed for a whole new cycle. He would pass the torch of the game to the boy. One hand to another.

"Just an old something I found in the basement. I thought you might find it handy. It won't make a winner of you, but perhaps it will give you an appreciation of the game. It was mine years and years and years ago when I played ball down on the Riverdale Flats. I thought I was Cap Anson then."

The boy undid the package. He stared at the glove.

The leather, once black, had tarnished to an antique grey. The sunlight and catches of archaic summers etched its skin with a myriad of lines. The look of a ready-for church shoe shine it once possessed, had faded to a dull patina. But the hide felt supple. It smelled of time, a basement scent, as if it had held its breath an aeon and exhaled a fragrance of musty rebirth when the boy opened and closed it before slipping it on.

The fingers that had reached for a hundred thousand flights were rounded and workman-like in their shape. Each digit fanned like the boughs of a tree, flowing from the hollow of the palm, as if it needed something to grasp, something unfinished and unfulfilled. A hunger.

To the smallness of his hand it felt vast inside, as broad and empty as a field at sunrise; yet the glove seemed magical and spread its fingers as if to fly. It wanted to speak. To tell a story. And it held all the seasons that time forgot, silently, secretly, as if sworn to an oath.

iii)

"Who is Cap Anson?" asked the schoolyard bully. The boy proudly displayed his glove to the gathered.

"Geez," answered the boy. "Don't you know?" The others marvelled. "He's the one who gave this to my Gramp. The glove is magical. It's a lucky glove." And because he had the glove, the bullies let him alone. There was something powerful and mysterious about the old black hand. Secretly, they envied him. He would toss a ball into the air and sometimes even catch it. The pock was electrifying.

The following Saturday it was raining hard. He wore a yellow sou'wester and black rubber boots, the glove tucked in his coat to keep it dry. The schoolyard was empty. A note tacked to the fence post bore the list of those on the junior Church team. In the pouring rain he scanned the roll. The words bled and ran together. His name was not to be found. He went home and put the glove in his closet. And there it sat, forgotten, for years.

The seasons counted off, odd, even, odd, even, like boys dividing up the gang for teams. He seldom thought of baseball. Instead, he studied hard. Math. Science. Eventually Physics. His legs lengthened and his shoulders spread. And by the time his Mother woke him one morning to tell him that his Grandfather had died, the boy looked at himself in the mirror and could hardly recognize the young man he'd become.

His Grandfather never asked him about the glove. An unspoken understanding was shared between them. If the subject of baseball arose in their talks, the old man would say "You'll grow into it someday."

"Did you ever dream of earning your living at ball?" the boy asked his Grandfather as the old man was dying. There was a long pause, a distant silence, as if the old man was somewhere else. The flats of the Don. A morning mist. A boy in knickerbockers, a penny-farthing bicycle against a tree. A hand digs deeply into the glove. He throws a fastball. It hangs there forever.

"Next time," he told the youth with a wink. "Always another spring."

iv)

"Your Grandfather would have been proud of you," his Mother said with a sigh as she packed his suitcases for University. Rummaging through his bedroom closet, she inspected each garment he could take away.

"What's this old thing?" she turned and asked. She held the glove.

The young man took it in his hands. A smile came to his face. He put his hand inside. The glove fit like a second skin. "This'll go," he said and tossed it on the bed.

The dusty summer was almost over as he stared from the window of his room in the dorm. A group of guys were out in the quad, tossing a baseball back and forth. He grabbed the glove and joined them.

"That's some mit there," said one of the gang as they sat cooling off in a booth at Barney's. Each in turn had a go at the glove, slipping their hands in, feeling its texture, flexing the spread. "How old is it?"

"Dunno," said the young man as he poured a round from the sweaty jug. "Belonged to my Grandad."

One of the guys rolled down four digits leaving the middle one up by itself, and held up the glove to a table of seniors. The elders pretended they hadn't noticed. "Can't do that with the nowadays mitts."

"Cut it out," said the young man. "My Grandfather was a gentleman. Respect it. Honour it. It's a lucky glove. It is magic."

"Yeah, right," said the joker. "Let's see how lucky you are with this thing. Baseball tryouts are next week. I'll bet you a jug you can't make the team with this relic."

The young man stared at his friend for a moment. This was a dare. A double dare. He'd never played baseball before. Real baseball. Back down now and the glove would be meaningless. Agree and flop and his reputation would crash. Try out and succeed was the only avenue.

"You're on," said the young man, and shook on the deal. And before he left, he dipped his fingers in the ends of the round and rubbed some draft on the glove's old hide.

v)

His heart was thumping. He burrowed his clenched fist into the deep hollow of the palm. Bent over, he waited for the ball. Concentration. Eyes on the plate. Watch the trajectory. He drew a bead on the object, placed himself in its path, and waited. A lifetime passed. The smack and sting sent lightning up his arm. His free hand dug into the mitt, came up with the ball and rifled the reply to second. The runner was dead on the tag. The Coaches pointed and spoke among themselves.

After the tryout, the young man sat in the locker room. He laid the glove beside him on the bench and wiped his face with a white towel. His hand still stung. He stared at his palm and turned it over. There, among the hair and sinews of the back of his hand, was a strange tattoo. A bruise? He looked closer. A backwards number 2 had inscribed itself with black ink on his flesh. He picked up the glove and stared down its throat. There, the grandfather had written his own name. The inscription was dated 1902.

The Coach came into the locker room and stood over him. "You've got a good shot, kid, but ditch the mitt."

A week later he paused by a bulletin board in the Athletic Center, and there on a list written in black ink, he found his name among the members of the new team. His assigned number was 2.

"You may think it was just natural manly ability," said the friend as he paid for the jug of draft, "but I figure it was that glove. Give me a go at making a wish on it. I've got a Macro-Ec test tomorrow." The young man tossed it over. Sure enough, his friend got an A. News spread.

All winter, through classes and exams, the young man dreamed of playing baseball. When he gathered on Fridays with his friends at Barney's, he would bring the glove, pass it around, and spend hours, sometimes, staring at the mitt. The glove became everyone's friend. Some touched it for good luck before a big date. Others, on the eve of a test or exam, would rub it under their arms and kiss its soft, dark flesh. And gradually, the young man who couldn't make the junior Church League team became known around the campus as "that guy with the lucky glove."

By the end of spring training, the young man couldn't wait for his first real game. The team boarded the bus and travelled several hours to the opponent's campus.

He was billeted in a dry, hot motel room with the Catcher, a senior, who snored like an overworked mill. In his state of exhausted semi-consciousness, the young man lay awake worried about how the lack of sleep would affect his play the following day. But by four a.m., the aria faded to a subtle whistle and sleep overtook the fielder.

He dreamt that he was standing in left field. The old glove was on his catching hand. The game was in late innings, the score tied, a runner at first. A batter who looked as if he could wallop the ball, came to the plate, knocking the dirt off his shoes with the tip of the bat. The pitch. The ball left the ash cleanly. It was hit directly to him and he was ready to call when suddenly the glove began to shake wildly on his hand.

"Mine!" yelled a voice at the end of his arm. The glove freed itself from his grasp. It stumbled to the ground where it spun round like a top, jumped into the air, caromed off the centrefielder who had come as back-up on the play. It shot into the air, twenty, thirty feet. Pock! It made the catch and flew like a bullet toward first where it slapped the bag emphatically, then turned and fired a cannonading blast to second where it scooped down and caught its own shot in the dirt and had the runner dead to sights on the slide. In a matadorial gesture, the glove flung itself with an "Ole!" into the air and opened up to let the Umpire inspect its feat. And there, cradled like an egg in the hollow of its palm, was the ball. The entire bench poured onto the field. Everyone gathered round to congratulate the glove. "Bet you couldn't have done that," said one of the players to the young man. "An unassisted double play!"

The team took the glove out for a beer. After several hours, the young man wanted to go home, but the glove wouldn't leave. Finally, he got fed up and left alone. Next day he heard a rumour that the waitress had gone home with the old mitt.

He woke with a start in the grey, stuffy motel room. He looked over at the night table, and there, in the darkness that came just before the dawn, he saw his wrist watch ticking away the seconds of his own life, and next to it the dark, mysterious outline of the glove.

vi)

With the team down by two runs and a man on first, the young man came to the plate. He'd gone down swinging in the third and sixth, but this time he knew it was going to be different.

En route to the on-deck circle he laid his new glove, an autographed tanned cowhide special, on the bench beside him. When he put his fingers to his nostrils to scratch away an itch, it was the scent of the future, not the past, that penetrated the core of his senses.

The count went one and three. The runner wanted to go. He swung. Bingo! The ball kept going. It stopped along the way and made a long distance call. "Don't hold dinner. I'll be gone awhile." A voice inside his mind demanded he concentrate: "make sure you step on all the bags," as he lapped the infield.

Regardless of his homer, his team still lost. "Where's that damn glove when we need it," some of them asked as he changed to his civies. But sometimes it even feels good to lose, the young man thought to himself, although one doesn't share that with the team. This was his moment. He was proud of himself. The magic was his, not the glove's. He was nobody's number two. The separation had been made.

He could have been sentimental about the old glove. After all, the thing had a history. Personal history. He could have held onto it, and loved it like a mourner who won't relinquish a corpse; but something in his relationship with the glove had changed. In the absolute sense, it had never been his. It was someone else's glove, contained someone else's dreams and hopes. This was his game now.

When the team bus finally pulled up to their campus, there was just time enough to catch the final round at Barney's. One last gulp to wash their sins away. He brought the old glove along for a last farewell, and laid it on the table as the barmaid served.

"Sexy glove," she said admiringly and stroked its supple leather.

"Yes," said the young man. "Its magic, you know."

"We could all've used some of that magic today," added a disgruntled teammate who'd booted a shoe-string catch in extra innings to send them home in defeat.

The young man stared up at the rafters above the table. A nail protruded from the beam. Suddenly, he jumped up and held the glove aloft. "Luck for everyone! Luck for the house!" he shouted and turned and hung the glove upon the nail. The entire bar applauded.

He goes into Barney's every now and then, and like all the regulars pays his respects to the glove. He toasts its magnificence, its mystery, its leather. Perhaps when he graduates he'll come back and fetch it and spread the luck around.

As he leaves, he turns and looks to that rafter. He tips his hat or nods goodbye. And the glove waits silently for another spring.

Goodbye Mr. Spalding

The tiki had a wry grin on its face as I tossed it from the poop. It spun through the air, head over heels, as the last rays of the beautiful sub-equatorial sunset caught it in a silhouette so that one stubby little deity arm was raised as if to wave goodbye. With a splat it hit the curling blue-green waters of the Pacific that rolled the little god onto its face like a drowning man. And all the while I was thinking: the little bugger is still smiling.

"Is that the lot of it Goodfriend?" asked Albert Goodwill Spalding as he clung tenaciously to the oak rail. The *S.S. Alameda* from San Francisco rocked gently back and forth beneath our feet. I nodded.

But that wasn't the lot of it. Far from it. I didn't want to say anything because, after all, I try to live up to my good name, and this mogul of the great game was my bread and butter, my ticket out and back, so to speak. At that moment, with my soup doing cartwheels in my gut, I wasn't in the mood for a full-blown tête-a-tête with Albert Goodwill himself.

Spalding stared at the sea like an ancient mariner. "I've briefed the boys and paid off the crew. Captain Morse will be mum. Nothing more will be said about our little Samoan adventure. American interests will remain intact, the stars and stripes will be proudly hailed by the dawn's early light wherever the great game is played. Now, I'm counting on you to do your best. Remember: God, baseball and manifest destiny." He gave me a playful little punch in the upper arm.

"What's Palmer saying about all this?" I asked. Palmer was a fellow journalist who had also signed on to cover Spalding's World Tour. At that moment, he was below deck having another literary catharsis into a galvanized bucket.

Spalding reached into the breast pocket of his pale linen vest and pulled out a piece of paper. "This'll be sent from Australia. By the time we get there, the boys'll have forgotten the whole thing. That's the great thing about ball players, you know." He cleared his throat. "December 1st...*Off* Samoa."

"Did you say *off?*" I couldn't believe my ears.

"Yes, *off*. As far as everyone's concerned we never landed. There was a terrible storm."

"Well," I replied with hesitation, "tossing some cheap tikis into the drink is one thing, but how do we explain the rudder? I mean, someone back in the States is going to spread the word about the broken rudder and how we put into Samoa for three days. And what about Robert Louis Stevenson? He's busy writing a book about the island. And the Samoans?"

"Who is going to believe the man who wrote *Treasure Island* and a bunch of heathen savages in grass skirts?" Spalding looked me resolutely in the eye like a bronze eagle atop a flag pole. "We're Americans, dammit, civilized men from the nation that represents the greatest achievement in human ingenuity. We're born to invent. Telephones. Steamboats. Democracy. We can invent whatever we want. How could anyone suspect us of lying? Be a good man and write your reports along the same lines as Palmer."

I wondered whether it was the sea that had felled Palmer or a pang of conscience. Spalding cleared his throat again as if he was about to make another speech. "This is what Palmer is saying, and I think it is highly suitable for our purposes: *We did not attempt to land but lay in the harbour a half mile from shore until two boats -- one a sloop and the other a little dory that bobbed about us like a cork on the waves--*"

"Pardon me? You mean we couldn't manouevre a full-fledged steamboat up to a pier, but a dory and a sloop made it through storm-high waves? That's incredible."

"Well, can you think of a better version, Goodfriend?"

"Yes, I can. The truth." I'd put my foot in it right there. I saw the Obituary desk of *The Chicago Herald* rising like a pillar of fire across the desert of my journalistic future. "But, of course," I hastened to add on second thought, "the truth is all a matter of how you look at it. Subjectivity? Right?" I smiled. I had visions of working as a sheep drover in Australia to pay my passage back. I hate sheep. Spalding glared at me, then he understood. It was a low-point in my journalistic career.

"Right." Spalding continued, "....*had come out from the dock with foreign mail and two passengers for Auckland. Had we reached...*and this is the part that explains why we had no souvenirs from Samoa "

"--Or why you had me toss them all overboard..."

"You catch the drift."

"So did the tiki...but continue."

"*Had we reached these islands in daytime, our ship would have been surrounded with canoes filled with natives and we should doubtless have been able to bring away with us many interesting relics of their country.*"

"I'm not even going to ask how the little boats found us in the darkness on a stormy sea."

"Goodfriend," said Spalding earnestly, "this is not about the truth; this is about baseball. We're in the process of building a new dream for people. If you mistake the game for the reality then there is no game, just the weight of the world on you." And he turned and walked away and left me standing there on the poop deck with the beautiful gold-green sub-equatorial sunset roaring away behind me.

But I have had the weight of the world on me. All these years. Everytime I roll a baseball in my hand and read the Spalding name on it I get pangs. The truth has been gnawing at me because I've always felt, deep down inside, that my business was to report the truth, or as much of it as I could chuck by an editor. Call it ethics. I prefer to name it reliability. I can't dignify a lie and call it a truth. That sort of thing is for people who write fiction, and that's another business all together, though I don't know how they live with themselves.

I wish to state for the record that I, Samuel Goodfriend, formerly of *The Chicago Herald* and lately of Peoria, Illinois, was witness to a fabrication and a falsification of the greatest magnitude, which was perpetrated by Albert Goodwill Spalding in order to hide the disgrace that the greatest baseball team ever assembled suffered at the hands of some Samoans in grass skirts.

The Pacific leg of the famous World Tour of 1888 didn't happen the way Palmer says in his book. Those natives were the greatest baseball players I have ever had the pleasure of witnessing on a diamond. I owe it to myself, and dammit anyways, I owe it to those bloody Samoans and their silly white-toothed honest grins because for a fleeting moment I saw something better than all our illusions and delusions about optimism and greatness. I saw the real thing. The real thing played with real heart, for honour and love and tradition, not for money or fame or vainglorious pride; and that spoke to me.

Events were set in motion one day in September of 1888. I was sitting in the owner's box at the old Chicago Grounds as the immortal White Stockings were squishing the Cleveland Spiders. The game was in late innings and the outcome wasn't in doubt. Not by a mile.

Some of the others in the assembled press gang were trying to butter Spalding up with remarks like "there are none finer" and "wherever would you find a crew of equals?" I'm not big on rhetoric, especially the empty, cloying stuff. The harder they blew the more he puffed up. I was sitting out the dance and trying to keep my mind on the game. And then, this devilish notion struck me. Don't ask me where it came from. It just popped into my mind.

"How do you know there are none better?" I asked out loud without taking my eyes from the field. "Have you bothered to check? I mean, have you scoured the world for a good game? How do you know that somewhere in the remotest corner of the bleakest desert or foresaken island, there isn't some lost civilization which invented baseball thousands of years before us and who have perfected the game far beyond any knowledge or understanding we have?"

The entire throng fell silent. They gave me the look: *now you've gone and done it*. Spalding tilted his head back and stared at the grandstand roof for a moment of sublime consideration. I am told that most men of genius strike that posture when they are confronted with the germ of a genuine eureka, and Albert G. had the act down pat. Instantly, he was struck by a great notion.

Spalding eyed the gathering. "Goodfriend's right, you know. How do we know there are none better? Have we scoured the world? Have we yet found our true match? Are there any out there, in the farthest flung reaches of the world's four corners who could match us and mate us? I think not. And what of those who have never ever witnessed the elegance of a double-play or the majesty of a homerun? What if we could spread the gospel of the game throughout the domaine of humanity? Would we then find our match?"

"Gentlemen," Spalding said, rising to his feet in a moment of greatness that some compared to Lincoln's delivery of the Gettysburg Address, "I propose a new venture for the Chicago White Stockings Athletic Club. A Baseball World Tour! We will take our great game around the world with us. We will enlighten the ignorant, we will cure the lethargic, we will awaken the bored. We will beat the daylights out of anyone who thinks they can play us! A World Tour of Baseball's finest!"

There was a round of applause from the reporters. Chicago scored another run. 15-2.

"But what happens," I added because I was enjoying this little tease of mine that had taken everyone by surprise, "if there is no team to play? I mean a real team. Say, for instance, you end up in some little community a day's jaunt from Timbuktu, and the only ones there who can remotely throw a ball and handle a bat are the local village idiots? What then? Would you have your Chicagoans beat up on them the way they're pulling the legs off the Spiders right now?"

"Goodfriend has a point," declared the great man after due consideration, and after careful financial forethought. "A Spalding team is always a fair team, because the Spalding name is the synonym for sportsmanship. Goodwill is my middle name! To this end, gentlemen, I also propose that we assemble an all-American team of the game's finest from other teams, and we take them along to beat up on instead of beating up on the locals!" There was more enthusiastic applause. Every head suddenly bent over a reporter's pad. Mad scratching all about. The bird had hatched.

My little jest sprouted wings and began to fly on October 20, 1888. Boys ran alongside the pullman and shouted support. Three cheers for Mr. Spalding! Women stood on the platform and waved goodbye. Our marvellously out-fitted railway carriage pulled out of the station in Chicago and headed west for a series of barn-storming raids on the sleepy cities of St. Paul, Cedar Rapids, Des Moines, and Hastings in Nebraska. As I sat amid the cigar smoke and air heavy with beer and bravado in the lounge coach, I wasn't sure whether I had signed on with the next chapter of Lewis and Clarke or the sequel to the Donner Party.

And no corner of the round world would be spared us. I was told how honoured I should feel that I'd been included in this great expedition, and for the most part I did feel pretty lucky. A year away from debts in Chicago, a whole twelve months without deadlines, and the prospect of wintering in the Australian summer made me happy. Join a paper and see the world.

As far as baseball was concerned, I would have the opportunity to hang out with the greatest names of the day. There was Cap Anson, Captain of the White Stockings, who would eventually make it all the way to Hall of Fame after an eternal career as a player and a manager. Pfeffer, Sullivan, Baldwin, Burns. They were all there for the Chicagoans. John Montgomery Ward, Ned Hanlon, Fred Carroll and Wood and Fogarty rounded out the All-Americans.

In Denver we added Cannonball Crane. Someone said he could throw a baseball a country mile, but I knew he had city written all over him. I hadn't noticed him at all at first, until he scared the daylights out of me in the lounge car when he let loose with the most amazing tenor voice. Donizetti, Schubert, Mozart, you name it. It was a long journey; he had a broad repetoire.

As predicted, the White Stockings destroyed the All-Americans everywhere they went. The All-Americans didn't seem to mind. After all, the pay was excellent, the booze was free. Personally, I would have a hard time looking myself in the mirror day after day if I knew I was brought on such a venture to be the resident victim. The White Stocking claim to being the world's best appeared to be a water-tight guarantee.

"Are there any among you who would like to challenge the game's best?" Spalding would ask from a soap box at each barnstorming event. You should have looked into the eyes of those farmers who had driven their wagons hard all night to venture from the hinterlands and the bleak remote parts of the wild west where only the silence and the hardship counted a man's heartbeats until his lifetime passed out of him with a painful sigh. To think they'd hauled hard, for days maybe, just so they could stand there in a crowd ten deep beneath the sweltering sun and witness magnificence. But that's the impact baseball was having on America in 1888. These were the faithful. The proselytized. I'm sure more than one of them went home and taught a son or two how to pitch a baseball. The tour had that effect on people. A.G. was a genius.

Things were going fine until we reached Colorado Springs. Game time came and Spalding took his head count. "Where is Montgomery Ward and that pitcher Crane?" hollered Spalding as his cheeks puffed and his face reddened.

Hanlon pointed to the hills. "Up there. They went riding as soon as the train got in."

Spalding turned to the mountains. He raised an accusing finger to the highlands. "Get down out of there and play ball!" he shouted.

And sure enough, not five minutes later, we saw a cloud of dust making its way along the road toward the fair grounds. The crowd parted. Two horsemen galloped in at a terrific speed. One looked every bit the cowboy with his hair flowing in the breeze and a free hand slapping his beast's rump. The other rider was hanging on for dear life, shouting, "I can't stop this thing!" He lapped the outfield and the crowd darted every which way. "Mad beast! Mad beast!" came his troubled cry.

The cowboy rider pulled his horse up in front of the mound and the animal reared up on hind legs. "Hi-O!" he shouted. The crowd applauded. It was Crane. He was still wearing his civies. Someone grabbed the reins as he dismounted and led the horse away. He brushed the dirt off his sleeve and walked calmly toward the mound as if nothing had happened.

The other horse was carrying John Montgomery Ward. His ride had turned into a wild-west show. The crowd started to stampede as his horse darted and spun with a manic frenzy. Rodeo. It spotted a gap near third base and headed for daylight with Ward calling over his shoulder "I'll be back in a minute!" He arrived in time to bat for the fourth inning. After this episode, Spalding, in a spirit of judicial fairness, pronounced a new rule: dressage riding only before a game.

Finally, we reached San Francisco. Spalding stood on a promontory where the bay emptied into the wide blue expanse of horizon. Palmer and I and the others were gathered there with note pads in hand to record the historic moment. And, of course, Spalding knew how to pose. He looked every bit like a conqueror. Alexander on the shore of the Bosphorus. Hannibal on the crest of the Alps. "There," he turned to us and pointed westward, "is no baseball." I had to agree. It was the Pacific Ocean.

We embarked the next morning on the steamer *S.S. Alameda* bound for Sydney, Australia by way of Hawaii and Auckland, New Zealand. I couldn't help but share Spalding's sense of dynamic optimism. We were Americans. We were taking America's game to the world. And who knew what would happen? "O brave new world that has such people in it," I thought in a flash of Shakesperean eloquence and reached for my notebook.

They feted us in Hawaii. But we hit a major snag there. The *Alameda* had been delayed by engine trouble on the leg west from Frisco, so that we arrived in Honolulu on a Saturday afternoon, too late to accommodate our scheduled game. Spalding was adamant: no baseball on Sunday. So, we departed the next day, having been grandly entertained but without having hit or pitched for almost two weeks. And you could tell that the lay off was bothering the players. There were daily workouts on the afterdeck and batting practices with a ball tethered to the mast. But that wasn't enough for the men.

So, when the Captain announced to us that we had lost our rudder and were drifting towards Samoa where we would have to put in for a few days while repairs were made, a cheer went up among the teams, and with eager gratitude for the opportunity with which fate had answered their prayers, they piled into the long boat and rowed ashore to claim Samoa in the name of Baseball.

A crowd gathered on the dock. They waved their arms and shouted with glee, and reached to touch us as we stepped from the long boat. The players immediately bought souvenirs and probably paid ten times the price for things. Tourists should never buy stuff off the dock like that. A rule of travel.

Spalding started to address the men and when the throng reckoned that he was the contingent's leader, they hoisted him aloft, festooned us all with garlands of flowers and carried him in procession to a grove of stately palms that offered shade and dignity beneath the scorching equatorial sun. In the middle of the grove, the locals had constructed a tall tower of bamboo laced together with viney thongs.

A spontaneous dance broke out among the natives around the base of the tower. "They know a hero when they see one," he turned to me and said. His straw hat, I thought, was getting tighter than usual. Spalding's eyes lit up. "What a grand gesture," he said to Ned Hanlon. "What a grand gesture in our honour."

A thin man with sunken cheeks, scraggly moustache and a Scottish accent stepped forward and introduced himself to Spalding and the other journalists who scrummed-in to catch every word.

"I am Robert Louis Stevenson," the Hibernian said and extended his hand. "Poet, author and traveller."

Spalding inflated. "I am Albert Goodwill Spalding. Owner of Spalding Sport Goods Company, the Chicago White Stockings Baseball Club, and Leader of this Grand World Tour of the Great Game." Spalding shook the writer's hand with vehemence. "I have read your work, Mr. Stevenson, and am a great admirer of yours."

"Really?" answered the surprised Scotsman and in a slightly flattered gesture bowed his head and touched his free hand to his breast. "*Treasure Island*, perhaps? Everyone has read *Treasure Island*."

"Nope."

"Ah, *Kidnapped*. *Kidnapped* is among my finest."

"Ah, no. Not that. Let me think." Stevenson removed his hand from Spalding's and put it in his pocket while the American pondered the answer to the question he had raised. "Let me think," mused Spalding. "Wait a minute. It will come to me. Uh...Yes! Now I have it. It is one of my favorite pieces of literature. '*How would you like to go up in a swing, Up in the air so blue? Oh, I do think it is the pleasantest thing...*"

"*That ever a child can do...*" added Stevenson in disbelief. "Anything else? *Travels with a Donkey*, perhaps?"

"No. Only that," replied Spalding. "Splendid piece of writing. Couldn't have said it better myself. You should forget about other things and write more stuff like that. Good show."

Stevenson's face was struck with an attitude of utter deflation. Spalding reached into the side pocket of his linen suit and pulled out a gift. "Here's a baseball, Mr. Stevenson. Has my name on it. Remember 'Only Spalding has real balls!' That's a slogan. You won't find any official balls that don't have my name on them. Consider it autographed."

Stevenson took the ball in his fingers, and sure enough there was the Spalding name. "Do you sign these personally, sir?" he asked coyly.

"Wish I had time. Wish I had time." Spalding leaned forward with an attitude of secrecy in his voice. "We're here to play baseball, but I don't imagine these heathens could comprehend such a divine gesture. Any exposition would probably be wasted on them. I guess all we'll do here is practice. Limber up the boys. No. I don't think ball's for these types."

The Samoans, however, were well within ear-shot. Spalding stood back and addressed them directly with a huge smile on his face. "Here. Play ball. Looky-see ball. Swish. Knock. Homerun. Baseball." He nodded. The crowd nodded back. "Not a word of English, eh? Bet they couldn't play a man's game."

"On the contrary, Mr. Spalding," Stevenson replied. "I've been here for several months now and have gained an infinite appreciation of these people. They are clever beyond my wildest expectations, and I do believe they are capable of anything."

"Well, they certainly know how to welcome an American hero!"

"You think this is for you?" asked Stevenson incredulously. "Why, no, they only carried you from the dock because they needed an audience for their contest. Pow-pow Kai has challenged Pow-pow Vree to a duel." Stevenson pointed casually to the top of the tower. "There they are now. See the tethers around their legs? The vines are just long enough to keep their heads from hitting the ground. They are going to jump together and whoever bounces higher on the rebound wins the argument."

"Good Lord, no!" retorted Spalding. "Heathens! Whatever would possess them to do that? They'll both be torn to bits. This is savage suicide."

"Possibly," replied Stevenson nonchalantly. "I'm not sure what the disagreement was about. Something mathematical, from what I've been able to ascertain from their debates on the matter. Something about twos and threes. It's a muddle, rather."

And with that the two parties in dispute leapt simultaneously from the tower, trailing behind them long cords of viney rope. And, as predicted, they fell to the full length of their tethers and were immediately snapped back into the air. One bounced higher than the other to win the argument.

The crowd rushed forward to cut them down. The loser suffered a broken leg and the indignity of having lost the argument. The winner had a fractured ankle and a huge smile on his face. They were both hustled away by the assembled audience, leaving the American teams standing there in shocked disbelief.

"Come," said Stevenson, "let me show you to a fine restaurant I've found just up the hill a little ways. It is run by a German couple. I recommend the *Coq au Vin*. But do avoid the Steak Tartar; it can be rather iffy in the tropics."

And good to his word, we had what we thought was the best meal on the Southern Pacific leg of the tour. Champagne all around. Crème brûlé for dessert. All in the middle of nowhere, on an island I hadn't known to exist before we rowed ashore that morning.

"And you know," added Stevenson as he wiped his mouth on the starched French linen serviette and graciously allowed Spalding to pay the bill, "the place is never over-booked."

"We will need a field in which to have a game. My men need to keep in shape. They are the best in the world, but they need to play," Spalding noted out loud in the hope that Stevenson would recommend a suitable clearing in the rainforest for a diamond. "You'll see to it."

But the Scotsman was peculiarly silent. There was something in Stevenson's eyes, a look I saw again when we went to England and beat the world-famous Marylebone Cricket team at their own game, which suggested that he had taken a dislike to Spalding. I anticipated irony.

I spent the afternoon strolling about on my own. I found a temple where it was obvious the locals were worshipping, not the moon and the stars, but their desire to travel there. They would fly about in strange masks and make as if they were flying through space. Very strange. Who would want to go to the moon?

I found the Samoans to be a wonderful people. If they see a stranger on the street, they will flash the most beautiful smile, grab you by the arm and lead you to their home where they will entertain you royally with pantomime attempts to explain what they want you to know. I had the feeling they thought I knew no language at all, and all I did was enforce that hunch because I figured that anything I could say in English would be wasted on them. So we pantomimed.

I was taken to one such hut and set upon a bamboo throne. My hosts must have noticed how I was staring at a household deity they had propped up in the corner. It was a wooden god. The word for it is "tiki". This one was grinning and reminded me of all the faces I saw about me. It had an arm up-raised, and at the end of it were broad, flat fingers which looked suspiciously like a baseball glove. I took off my necktie and offered it to them in exchange for the carving, and to my surprise they accepted the deal immediately. And that is how I came by the tiki.

We returned to the Alameda for dinner, but by that evening half the team was lined up for the washrooms. The head, they call it. By morning, some were too sick to leave their cabins, let alone go ashore for a practice or a game. Still available for service were Anson, Hanlon, Crane, Pfeffer, John Montgomery Ward, Fred Caroll, George Wood, Baldwin and Daly -- a mix from both squads. The rest ate the tartar.

"We'll go at ten and have a full practice," Spalding declared over breakfast. And again the team rowed ashore. I had used part of the previous day to do some sight-seeing. You have no idea how beautiful an island like Samoa can be on the first of December. Unlike the northern climes of Chicago, the flowers were in rich bloom; flamboyant trees, bougainvillaea, camellias. The air was like a lady's dressing table with its rich perfumes. The abundance of colour, the blue skies and stunning blossoms reminded me of paradise. "Yes," I thought to myself, "these people know a thing or two to live here." And know a thing or two they did.

As our boat put into the dock, a contingent of natives was waiting for us. Stevenson was acting as their spokesman.

"Good morning Mr. Spalding," shouted the Scotsman as he helped the team disembark. "I have a proposition for you from the locals. They want to challenge you to a game. Baseball anyone?"

"My men are in no condition for a game. They have come down with food poisoning."

"Ah, the steak tartar. Well, I can't say I didn't warn you." Stevenson took a quick headcount of the Americans. "I say, what with my limited knowledge of the game, you do appear to have enough to field a squad. And we have more than enough players here if you need some bench strength. Perhaps we can loan you some of the Samoans."

"Totally out of the question," Spalding fired back. "We do not play with savages."

And at that juncture, the devil got in me again. I took Spalding's arm and pulled him aside. "Perhaps," I interjected cautiously, "a game would be good. Baseball might just click here. The competition is... well, you realize that they won't slide because of their grass skirts. Not if they are the least bit, well, manly, so to speak. And besides, it would make great copy for the papers. SPALDING PROSELYTIZES THE HEATHENS TO OUR NATIONAL SPORT. White Man's burden. That sort of thing. It would sit well with the missionary set who think baseball is next to dancing on the list of all-time evils." Spalding nodded and gave the matter consideration for a moment. He stepped forward again to resume the parlay.

"Mr. Stevenson," he said, "we accept your challenge. Give me nine good Americans anytime, and we will take on the world. A friendly game," he said turning to wink at me. "After all, Goodwill is my middle name." And so the die was cast.

We were led to a clearing in a grove of mangos where a diamond had been laid out according to the proportions of Cartwright's Knickerbocker game. A prosperous-looking mound rose in the navel of the infield, and the outfield looked as well-groomed and manicured as those in the majors back home.

"They spent an entire night hacking this out of the bush," noted Stevenson as he waved his arm in a grand arching gesture of explanation. "It is amazing what these people can do."

"They did this all for us?" asked Palmer and took note on pad.

"I didn't say last night," Stevenson answered cryptically.

And there, lined along the first base foul-line like a visiting team in the senior circuit, was the Samoan starting line-up.

Stevenson introduced them: "At First Base, Pow-pow Mee; the Second Baseman Pow-pow Mai; Short stop Pow-pow Ya; playing Third, Pow-pow No; Left Field we have Pow-pow U, Center Field is Pow-pow Ay and Right Field is Pow-pow Hmm; Catching today's game is Pow-pow Uh. Pow-pow O will pitch. There's the lineup. I believe Visitors go first. Play ball, gentlemen. Pow-pow Kai and Pow-pow Vree would have given anything to be here today, but, as you know, they are on the disabled list. Pity, really, as Pow-pow Kai has tremendous speed and plays a good game at short."

I took Stevenson aside. "That land-diving thing yesterday..."

"You mean when they were settling an argument?"

"Yes. What was the cause of that?"

"Glad you asked, old fellow. Glad one of you is paying attention. They were arguing over who had more doubles and who had more triples."

"Baseball?" I asked incredulously.

"Well, not really. You see, Pow-pow Kai claimed he had more triples than Pow-pow Vree's doubles. To make such a claim here, according to local etiquette, is tantamount to an insult. They decided to settle the matter with a little land-diving. Shame, really, as Pow-pow Vree was excellent at blooping loopers into deep right or centre and almost always got a double. He'll probably increase his swing now, perhaps widen his stance a bit and keep his head up. He was a head-down style hitter. He sees the ball well. A few games of adjustment and he should be knocking the cowhide with the best of them, don't you think?"

My mouth must have fallen open. "Pardon me? Is it baseball or isn't it?"

"Well, I shouldn't call it that," Stevenson explained. "They have a name for it here. *Pow-pow Wham*. Named after some great ancestor of theirs who saved the game in the wake of a great scandal. They've been playing it for thousands of years. It's their national sport."

"I thought you told us that they hacked this diamond out of the jungle in a single night so they could learn the game?"

"Oh, you Yanks do get things twisted. No. I said that they hacked this diamond out of the jungle in a single night. That was three hundred years ago during a religious festival frenzy of some sort. They've cared blessedly for the place ever since. This is holy ground. They are playing today for the glory of their gods and the honour of their ancestors. They just aren't tripping about to show off."

A lump came to my throat. I looked over at Spalding. Had we brought lambs to the slaughter? He was pep-talking his side. It would be shameful to pull out now. The question remained: should I warn him? It was going to be a long day. Our opponents were tossing the ball about for warm-up with considerable velocity. The Samoans were ringers.

Hanlon came to the plate first. The Samoan stood on the mound, smiling that beautiful smile I'd seen everywhere. Hanlon called back to the bench, "Should I toy or teach?" Everyone yelled back "teach." The pitch came. It smoked him as he whiffed. Hanlon's eyes grew wide. "O!" he exclaimed. The pitcher nodded and smiled.

Spalding looked at his line-up card. "Don't encourage him!"

"What?" asked Hanlon.

"His name is Pow-pow O."

Hanlon stood in again. A curve came low and outside, but Hanlon reached and made contact. A lofting shot headed lazily to centre. "Ay," Hanlon cried at the sting of the bat in his hands. Ay moved forward and made the catch.

"A called shot!" expostulated Stevenson from his bench. "Very well done."

"What happened?" asked Hanlon on returning to the American

dugout.

"The Centrefielder's name is Pow-pow Ay. You put it right to him. He didn't even have to call for it!" Spalding looked up and down the bench. "No more grunts, groans, ugs, moans or interjections from anyone. You'll only be helping them."

Through three the game was scoreless. Spalding's men were beginning to sweat. They'd thrown their best stuff at the Samoans, and incredulously, the Samoans seemed to glide from play to play as if they were just warming up for the day. They didn't even seem to be trying. Fastballs. Diving shoe-string catches. We'd get a hit. We'd lay off the next stuff and walk. There'd be two men on and, *voila!* we'd hit into a perfect double play.

In the fourth, we had a rally going. The Samoans still hadn't scored. It was time to put the game away, to make a statement, to send a message. The bases were loaded. Hanlon in to bat. He drove a shot directly back at the pitcher. The pitcher, Pow-Pow O, turned and fired the ball to first like a gunshot to bag Hanlon.

Pfeffer began to depart second, hesitated, and tried to hold up. Pow-pow Mee at first rifled the ball back to the pitcher. Pfeffer began to move. But the second baseman, Pow-pow Mai, had slipped behind him and the pitcher, Pow-pow O, caught him with a direct hit. Pfeffer was dead on the tag as he headed toward third. Crane, who stood in stunned surprise at third, started to run toward home, but the third baseman, Pow-pow No, took off with him, and when the ball had been returned to the pitcher, it was a short quick underhand toss to the fleet third baseman who instantaneously tagged Crane. Spalding stood up, a horrified look on his face. His pallor paled.

"What is that?" he shouted with the fury of an angry god. He turned and glared at me. "Goodfriend! What on earth was that?"

"I believe that's what you call an O-Mee-O-My-O-No triple play." I simply held up my score card. He took it in his hands and his mouth fell open. We were in serious trouble.

Crane did his best on the mound. But they even hit stuff thrown high and inside or low and outside by a mile. Inning by inning the score mounted while our side was shut down. In desperation, alone and looking rather silly on the mound as pitch after pitch was hammered out and about, Crane let loose in his beautiful tenor voice. The rest of the team began to join in. It was like a ship going down:

Abide with me; fast falls the eventide,
The darkness deepens; Lord, with me abide:
When other helpers fail, and comforts flee,
Help of the helpless, O abide with me!

Pow-pow O threw incredible curves. They would head left then veer sharply right as they crossed the plate. Some shots dipped while others rose. There didn't seem to be any physics at work in Samoa.

Daly tried to chase down a ball at the edge of the outfield as it rolled into some beautiful orange flowers. A Samoan woman came running up to him. "Not in the sacred *la-las*!"

"Ay!" Spalding shouted as the Centrefielder crossed the plate. "Uh!" he cried in despair as the Samoan Catcher came in to score.

"Spalding! You've got to stop encouraging them," all of us insisted.

Daly looked stunned. While the entire team waited, he was having an anthropology lesson. "The *what-was*?" By the time he had heard a legend and grasped their significance, the base paths had cleared. "I heard the most amazing story," he said as he sat down on the bench and repeated the epic tale to others.

There is mercy in all civilized sports. The inventors of *Pow-pow Wham* or baseball foresaw our suffering when they limited a blowout to nine innings. The game ended in the bottom of the ninth when Baldwin popped up and left Anson stranded at third. Samoans 12, Americans 3.

Pow-pow O came over to our dugout. I thought it was a moment of supreme sportsmanship, but our leader read the situation differently. He walked up to Spalding. "Thanks awfully for a wonderful game, old chap."

Spalding wheeled around. Thunderbolts shot from his eyes. "You lousy, good-for-nothing cheats! You never told me you played ball!" said Spalding who was now totally red in the face and looking as if he might have a stroke.

"Now, now, Mr. Spalding. Remember. *Noblese oblige.* Sportsmanship. Goodwill is your middle name. Besides, you never asked. We have been playing our game for a thousand years here, and we like to think we've perfected the art. The thought of a World Tour never dawned on us. After all, we never stop to worry about who's the best. For us, it isn't a matter of competition. We play for the love of the game, and we were so pleased and honoured that you could demonstrate the finer points of the American game to us during your sojourn on our island. Thank you ever so much, old boy. We learned a great deal. We are eternally grateful."

"Liars!" shouted Spalding. Things were getting pretty serious now. Goodwill was glancing around at his feet for a bat.

"Whatever do you mean?" asked Pow-pow O, totally bewildered. The other Samoans had gathered round the American bench.

"You just bloody well stood there and never let on that you played ball."

"On the contrary," said Pow-pow O reflectively. "You assumed we were simpletons. In fact, you assumed we didn't even speak English. May I introduce you to Pow-pow Uh. Merton College, Oxford. Class of '81. M. Litt., superannuated."

Spalding turned to his team. "Let's go." We beat a hasty retreat to the dock, followed all the way by the happy crowd of locals. To make matters worse, all along the way, the throng kept asking for our autographs. Of the many things I learned that day, one is that defeated players hate to sign autographs.

We piled into the long boats. Some of our equipment even got left behind. Pow-pow O came running along the dock with Stevenson. "What should we do with your things? We'd be ever so pleased to bring them out to you."

"Never mind," hollered Spalding. He turned to the players who had taken up oars. "Pull! Hard! Harder!" Ned Hanlon tugged on his oar and the long boat slipped its moorings and bobbed up and down in the amethyst blue surf. The assembled multitude who had come to see us off raised their arms in the air and waved farewell.

As the dock and the happy crowd grew smaller and smaller in the distance, Pow-pow O who had pitched such a masterful game, jumped forward from the gathering and called after us in a phrase I have heard so many times since: "He's going, going, gone! Goodbye Mr. Spalding!"

Everytime a homerun is hit those words haunt me. In my profession, that's daily. And they come to haunt me every night in my sleep when I dream of a beautiful tropical island and a people who have refined a game so much like ours to a level of excellence that will take a thousand years to equal.

I dream of them running the bases. I see their pitches dipping and curving and kissing the corners of the strike zone. And I know that I have seen the future. If baseball manages to survive my countrymen, their hubris and their greed, I know it will be played, someday, with excellence.

Spalding did not turn to look at his admirers. Americans never look back. There would be other games to win. This one could be easily forgotten thanks to a bit of backtracking and the amnesia of history. *E Pluribus Unum*, untarnished, still perfect. We slid away from Samoa on the newly repaired *S.S. Alameda* and looked to rewriting two days of our lives to accommodate the angels of our lesser nature.

But, as I said, the truth has been burning a hole in my conscience. Genius, after all, needs its due. And that day in Samoa, I saw baseball genius. Magic. A love of the game. They were playing not to create an identity, but because they had one. And next stop? Who knows? Maybe they will go to the moon. Ha.

And I learned something about my countrymen. Their enthusiasm, their restless energy, their need to win -- the identity of a young nation -- was really the product of envy. And if anything or anyone proved better than they were, they would go away and sulk, rethink, retool, and come back again and again until they succeeded. And if the earth ever proved too bland a scope for their intentions, there would always be the moon, the stars, and whatever lay beyond.

As for Spalding, he refused to recognize *Pow-pow Wham* for what it was. But others on the team, Anson, Hanlon, who went on to successful managerial careers in the majors, they kept note. You can see Samoa written all over Hanlon's Brooklyn team of 1900, The

Superbas. Wee Willie Keeler was on that team. They won the World Series.

Perhaps that's also why Anson's career lasted as long as it did. I once saw Eddie Cicotte throw what I swore was a Pow-pow O inside curve. He should have used it in the 1919 Series. I even heard a rumour that Christy Mathewson spent the winter of 1902 in Samoa. I'd believe it.

Spalding blamed the debacle on cricket.

He was convinced that Stevenson had applied Cricket techniques to the Samoan game. "Mooglies" he would rant as he paced up and down with his namesake between his fingers in an attempt to work out the grip. I listened to his soliloquy about how Cricket would corrupt America's national sport. How the Devil himself had invented Cricket.

But he, Albert Goodwill Spalding, would get even. He would level the field. So, when we reached Australia, he set the wheels in motion. He consulted every Cricket expert in the country and trained the men to pitch and bat a century or more. Mooglies all round.

When we reached England, Spalding was the proudest man on earth when his White Stockings and All-Americans punished the world-renowned Marylebone Cricket Club at their own game. Getting even means getting up early. That's what legends are made of. Spalding was an early riser.

And when that creaky little tiki hit the waves, I had a thought which has never left me all these years. The idol's right arm was raised. It could have been waving goodbye, but it resembled a centrefielder making a climbing catch against the wall. Its splayed fingers were like a glove. Yes. It was reaching up. It was reaching to snag a high fly ball nibbling at the fence-top of a great, wide-open field. "Give me your best shot," the tiki seemed to say.

"Yes," I thought. "We will catch them. Just give us time."

The Death of Grass

"You can believe anything you want,"
they told him on his way up to the show:
he chose to believe in grass—the green sea
that washes over time when a pop fly hangs
like a lover's promise in an arc through centre;
the continent of pain when inches give way
to miles on the tip of a glove; the reach

that will always be bigger than a man;
the cool green smell of life itself
smiling up at the innings of August heat,
and the green that shone beneath the lights
like a sea of emeralds awash in voices.
Eight seasons he learned that faith is fortune;
balls never bounce the same way twice;

that even when you are under the ball
the wind can shift and change a game;
that all you tell others is less than you know;
that winning the Series is better than sex
though winning the Series will get you sex;
in playing the game you are playing yourself;
that baseball is poetry without the poet;

that the heart and body can be at odds;
that fortune falters when faith is shaken.
And you can believe anything you want—
and then, like a lover who suddenly leaves,
that season when you swing and miss,
swing again and whiff again, error in the ninth

on a pop fly, slip on a misplayed catch,
and watch from the bench as age prevails.
And then came the season they laid the rug.
"For a more even game," the owners said—
but the death of grass was the death of belief:
"You believe what you want, but never this,"
he said in farewell, his eyes rained out.

He sat one night in a ballplayer's haunt,
drinking slow beers and smoking fast drags.
A game was on the tube. A rookie. A fly ball.
An error scored. The game never gets better
and it never gets worse. The faces change,
parks are revamped, and always there, high
in the stands, the father, the son, the dream.

The lights are down now as he stands
at the plate, his face to deep centre
and the stars high above him like signals
called from eternity. There are no certainties
in this game—only believers who swing
at something hurled split-fingered out of forever,
and sunlight on grass as green as last year.

The Summer Is Over

It's sad to admit it ends so soon,
but everyone knows those are the lucky ones.
Most guys are washed up by seventeen.
           Stuart Dybek, "Death of the Right Fielder"

"Fifth row, right behind the screen. Such stuff as dreams are made of. Do you know what it took to get these? Under normal circumstances I would have had to offer my first born. First born!" said Mike.

Roger took the tickets in hand. He held them up. "The Grrrr-ayy-ell! Your old man is very, very well connected. How about another?"

Roger leaned across the breadth of his room and opened the tiny Frigidaire where a row of Budweisers stood stolidly at attention in their wintery sleep. The clock of Bloor Street United chimed noon in the distance and Mike stood from the desk-chair and stared out the window. He had a far away look in his eye.

Jays versus Twins. Clancy pitching. The call of the Ex beckoned. The CNE would be going full-tilt with one last gasp of summer frenzy. The Midway. The beer gardens. Tiny Tom Doughnuts. Mike held out the tickets for display.

In the small room pasted with posters of ball players and pin-up girls, the two young men sat having a cold beer before heading off on their jaunt. It was a chance for both to savour the last fleeting moments of a time in their lives when the world turned on the possiblities and surprises of a single instant. This was the last day of what had been a marvellous summer and the end of a marvellous time of their lives. They had graduated together on a hot day in June and slaved together the entire summer on the loading platform of an auto parts company down by the Canary Restaurant.

Tomorrow, they both realized, things would change. Roger would be lining-up outside the School of Graduate Studies at nine a.m. to register for a new degree. Mike would be following the path of the awakened dead on a sleepy trudge to a King Street office tower where he would start the first day of a real job. At that moment, if both of them had had a wish, they would have asked that time stand still. They were almost twenty three. The summer was over.

"And," added Mike as he turned with a look of mock delight in his eyes, "I have a bit of extra something here to see us through the late innings when they turn off the beer." He reached into his jean shirt pocket and flashed the top of a silver flask.

"*Cabrone!*" delighted Roger. "You think of everything."

"Of course," smiled Mike. "A master at work."

Mike glanced at his watch. "T'is time. Beam me up Scotty."

"Ay, Captain."

As they made their way through the halls of rough mock-stucco walls, past the grungy brown doors that issued smells of onions and cabbage and failed student meals, Roger turned to Mike.

"Will you miss the old place now you can afford something better?"

"You're going to help me move in October," replied Mike. "Its hernia time," he said as the door to the old rooming house closed behind him. "But my little crawly powder-munching friends in the sink aren't coming with me. No pets allowed where I'm going. No one to share my left-overs."

The maple trees of the Annex were full and dusty beneath the Labour Day sun. They walked quickly along Bloor Street and the sunlight glinted off the windows of the shops. Everyone was out and about for the holiday, pushing strollers, hanging out in sidewalk dives, soaking up the last liberty of summer. At Bathurst the two amigos piled onto the street car and the vehicle shunted slowly southward, jerking to stops, gliding forward and halting again.

"My liquid annuity is going to come due," said Mike.

"As mine," added Roger. "With interest. Pray for green lights."

But soon enough, though not soon enough, the whalish streetcar pulled past the Princes' Gate and the noise of the midway wafted through the open windows as everyone piled off. They proudly displayed their *billet doux* at the turnstiles and in an instant they had left the real world far behind. Ex time.

After a quick pit stop in the Coliseum, they wound their way through the labyrinth of cotton candy and caramel corn stands, through the stalls of try-your-luck games, pausing only to stop for an instant at the pitch and toss where a muscle-bound man in a tank top was setting the order down to impress a fluffy-haired girl who bounced and jumped as she clapped with glee.

Mike slapped down two dollars on the counter. Roger looked at his watch. "We're going to miss the national anthem, Mike. You know how I hate to miss the national anthem. You know how I love the bad renditions and the failed high notes. We're going to miss the national anthem and the first pitch."

"Nag, nag," replied Mike. "We've got time. Besides, you know how they go." Mike began humming "The Star Spangled Banner." He took the balls from the carny. The target was a row of round-faced leather lions. The first pitch took out one of the smiling cats and it tumbled backwards as if it had been killed. Mike stood up straight from his follow-through, impressed with his prowess. He did a Satchel Paige wind-up for the second, but someone brushed his arm and his balance waivered.

"Balk!" hollered Roger.

"Will you cut it out? Can't you see I'm trying to do something very important?" He threw the pitch and took out the next lion. "There. Two in a row. Mustard time." He eyed the target. He put all he had into it. Too much, perhaps. The ball missed by six inches. "Let's go," said Mike in disgust. He pointed to the row of smiling lions. "Get you next time."

As the two hustled toward the stadium Roger asked "What would you have done with a stuffed dog if you'd won it?"

"Bought it a beer," came the reply.

They were in the corridors of the diamond stand. Everytime they passed the daylight of a passage, Roger would peer along the shute. "There are the anthems now," he said in disgust as they lined up at the beer counter and the tender carefully pulled the drafts into plastic cups to avoid foaming the issue. They were still three back when the announcement came over the speakers: "Leading off for the Twins..." They came away with two beers each. They calculated these would last until the third.

"The problem with this place is that the Fun Police are out in force. The U.S. parks like Yankee Stadium are so civilized," Mike said as they showed their stubs to the usher and were escorted to their angelic thrones five rows behind home plate. "In the American parks they bring the beer to you. You don't even have to get up from your seat. I call that civilized."

"They make you work for it, don't they. Fun Police rule numero uno: you can't have too much fun."

The crowd hollered. Minnesota had a man on. He was stealing second. Clancy turned and watched, but shrugged it off and the lead-off man slid toward Garcia in a cloud of dust.

"Ah, c'mon," Roger screamed in pained disgust. "The first guy up steals. A bunch of last-place bottom feeders and Clancy starts the game with a walk and then follows that by allowing a steal! He could at least have hit him with a pitch."

A man to Roger's right leaned over. "That's how it began. He hit the batter." Roger and Mike winced in unison. "Is the fix in?" the man laughed to himself.

"What did he mean by that?" Roger whispered to Mike.

"1919 World Series. The first batter was hit to signal the fix in the Black Sox scandal. Down here in the expensive seats, people know their ball."

"So, is he saying that Clancy's crooked or something?"

"Of course not, *dumkopf*, it was a joke."

Clancy got out of the inning and the Jays came to bat. Leading off was the shortstop Alfredo Griffin, followed by Damo Garcia and Dave Collins. Collins was worth the wait that season. The outfielder lent a spark of promise to the Jays. The previous winter they'd traded their leading hitter, Bonnell, to Seattle. Everyone said "go figure."

Mike and Roger considered themselves members of the brotherhood of suffering whose numbers included every Toronto ball fan. Things were beginning to happen. Bobby Cox had arrived two years before and the team had started to improve. The year before the Jays finished fourth. Now they were second.

In any other time or place, that second would have been an impressive first. But this was the year of the Tigers. They had begun hot. They'd stayed hot. No one was going to catch Sparky Anderson's record-setting crew. Just when they thought the bluebirds had a shot, hello! The fun police showed up. The brotherhood of suffering continued.

Patience became a civic motto.

The two amigos hadn't been in time to grab tickets to the Jay's first home opener against the White Soxs, the 'Snow Bowl' it had been called, but they had skipped school the next day and sat bundled in the stands when the dark clouds of an almost winter/almost spring descended upon the lakeside park and the losing began in earnest. But like a million other ball fans in Canada, they claimed they had been there when the first pitch was thrown.

As they had matured into manhood, or as close to it as they could be at that moment, they had watched their expansion franchise dawdle in the basement. Just when they thought there were no further ways to lose, the Jays found new ways to push the envelope. Roy Lee Jackson singing the national anthem and then throwing away a game. Joey McLaughlin. The loss of Pete Vuckovich to Milwaukee the season before he won the Cy Young Award as best pitcher.

But there were bright spots as well. A young shortstop up from Syracuse, Tony Fernandez, was a real comer. And there had been the steadfast Ernie Whitt who put his heart and soul into every game. Dave Stieb could be an all star if he had the hitting to back him up. Next year was always hovering just around the corner. Baseball in Toronto was a game of patience.

By the second, the game opener beers, which they had both stored so lovingly beneath their seats, had run dry. Mike volunteered for the sortie. "Wish me luck," he said as a thousand others headed with him to the tunnel.

Roger sat there and took in the day. The animal stands, the old CNE Grandstand, were chock to capacity and shook beneath the rhythmic stomping and cheering.

Roger stared at the netting of the foul screen. "This is what fish must see just before they are caught," he thought to himself.

The sky had silvered over as Cliff Johnson came to the plate. The Designated Hitter for the Jays had powerful arms. He'd become another favorite; there was so much to cheer for with this club. And just when it looked like they might put it all together, there was that annoying Detroit thing happening. Toronto luck.

Johnson whiffed with a big league cut.

The beautiful thing, Roger considered, was that these seats were so close you could hear everything the players said. Johnson said a dirty word.

Mike was still gone with the beer. What could be keeping him? Seagulls hovered lazily over the outfield. You could see the frantic motions in the stands over first base when the vermin swooped low for a bombing run.

"Yes," thought Roger, "the Old Ex is a grand place." He recalled, with fondness, sitting high over first base as the sun set into an orange sky behind the Ontario Government Building, a vision which reminded him of a postcard of a tropical cathedral someone had once sent him from Puerto Rico. The CNE was a strange place to play ball. It could be beautiful on hot summer nights beneath the stars when the lake breezes came in and offered assuring respite from the humidity. And other times it could be the cruelest park in the majors, damp and bone-chilling and absurd, a football field cut in half, and the empty seats of the Grandstand always looming over the outfield fence like someone's grave mistake.

At that moment, a squirrel darted across the field from first base. It tore off into the outfield as the players moved in with their gloves low to try to corale it. It did a frantic one-eighty and went lickety-split over the mound, across homeplate and up the screen where it clutched its paws to its chest in absolute terror. There it sat, panting, caught between life and death, the game and the spectators. Some of the softer-hearted observers uttered sounds like "awh" and "poor thing". Someone yelled out "Did the squirrel buy a ticket?" There it sat.

Mike returned to his seat and handed Roger a beer. "They'd only let me have two. Measly two. Fun Police. A curse on their houses. And you wouldn't believe the line-ups in the washrooms. Brutal! I'll be glad when they finally do something and build a real baseball stadium."

Roger smiled. "Maybe the squirrel can get you two more," he said and pointed to the screen.

Mike stared in amazement. The squirrel stared back. "Isn't that special," laughed Mike as he swilled from his plastic cup.

A Minnesota batter fouled back. The squirrel leapt into the air and landed back on the field. The chase began again. The crowd was roaring.

"Don't you think its overly cute that Toronto chose a squirrel as its Sesquicentennial mascot?" asked Roger.

"Surreal, more like it," replied Mike.

The creature darted through the legs of a policeman and ran into the Jay's dugout. "Surreal. Probably gone to suit up with Minnesota in the lead." Everyone awaited the squirrel's return. It was not to be.

Roger went out next and came back with a pair of cold ones. In the next inning, Mike went. And so they alternated, inning by inning. The sky grew more hazy.

The Twins and the Jays were tied in the bottom of the eighth, 3-3. But Clancy, who had done a reasonable job, vermin on the field and all, was tired. He walked two men. Bobby Cox slowly wandered out to the mound. There he held a conference and turned toward the bull-pen and tapped his right arm.

"Who the hell is going in?" shrieked Mike.

Dave Stieb, a starter, trotted merrily from the bullpen. "Why would Cox waste Stieb, on a relief assignment? Geez."

The man sitting next to Roger leaned over again. "Stieb's been injured lately, don't you read the papers? He's coming off some rehab. Cox probably thinks he needs the work to keep him in shape."

"But he's a starter," the two friends said in unison. The ball was given to Stieb. Restless murmuring swept through the stands. Stieb wound up. The ball left his fingers. It hit the bat. It left the park. A moan of Biblical proportions arose from the Labour Day crowd.

"That's it. I'm supporting the Red Sox next season," said the man next to Roger who excused himself and shuffled through the mass of legs to the steps. Everyone started to head to the exits. Roger and Mike held fast.

As the announcer thanked everyone for coming out and rubbed salt into the wound by noting that the final score was Twins 6 Jays 3, Mike and Roger finally stood and headed for the exits.

"Where to now, amigo?" asked Roger.

Mike pointed down. "The Longest Yard. They'll be open now for the post-game crowd." And so they went to the Longest Yard. They ordered more beers.

"Ah!" crooned Mike as he took a sip. "Long, long time since the seventh. Only in Toronto would they turn off the beer at a critical moment."

The sky was a grey overcast by the time they finished up several more beers and stepped outside. A few remnants from the Air Show were hopping about the sky. The two amigos stumbled over to a park bench to watch the dance of the airplanes.

A tiny Cessna was doing loop-the-loops above the lake. A woman pushing a child in a stroller stopped in front of them and pointed to the clouds. She spoke in an English or South African accent.

"Thay're's Murdoch." She traced the path of the airplane in the sky for the child. The child's eyes followed her finger. "You kn-yow Murdoch? Thay're's Murdoch." Suddenly, the plane's engine sputtered and cut out. The tiny white wings tumbled out of control and hit the lake with a crash as tail and wheels flew every direction on impact.

The woman with the stroller bent down to the disinterested child. "Thayat *was* Murdoch," she said and calmly pushed on as if nothing had happened. Roger and Mike sat stunned, their eyes wide. A crowd raced to the water's edge and people began to holler.

"Let's get out of here," said Mike and they headed for the Midway. Bruce Springstein's voice was bellowing out "Pink Cadillac" as the rides spun round and round and the lights glittered like jewels in the silver air. They were in front of the pitch and toss again.

"Try your luck," the man said. Mike bought three pitches.

"Snarky bastard lions, think you can fool me this time," he said and went into this wind-up. Mike closed his eyes, just as the carny stepped in front to retrieve a ball. Mike hit him squarely in the shoulder and the ball glanced back into the Midway.

"Sonnuvabitch!" hollered the carny, who leapt over the counter and took off after Mike and Roger. But the two amigos soon outdistanced their foe and lost him among the maze revellers.

Mike reached into his pocket and pulled out the silver flask. "Need a bracer after the chase," he said. They both took swigs.

"What is this," asked Roger?

"Napoleon Brandy. V.S.O.P. Only the best, eh?"

"In your face, sir."

They lined up and bought a strip of tickets and headed right for a ride which flung cages into the air and pulled them, with startling force, directly back down to the earth.

"No! Not that," exclaimed Roger with trepidation as Mike pointed to the mechanical beast.

"Why not? Remember our Canadian Lit class? That scene in *Under the Volcano* where the Consul General goes for a ride after imbibing a considerable amount of tequila? Well...?"

"Insanity," said Roger, over and over again as the attendant buckled them in to the tiny cage. Mike sat directly behind with Roger in front. "I'm going to die with an insane man screaming in my ear."

The ride went into motion. Of course, Mike screamed in Roger's ear. By the time the hearing had come back, Roger felt the bruise marks on his shoulder where Mike had dug in his hands in total fear. Time seemed to stand still.

The next thing they knew, they were sitting in the arena of the Coliseum and finishing the last drops of the brandy. The jumping competition was underway. A rider and mount with two faults trotted elegantly from the ring and the rider tipped his hat to the judges. The horse hung his head in shame. The next competitors were announced.

A rider in a black habit appeared at the gate with a huge white horse beneath him. The animal's veins and muscles bulged with power. They were announced. But as the rider dug in his heels as a signal to begin, the horse reared up suddenly and threw its rider. It tore wildly around the ring, hurdling over the rails and coming to a stop in front of Roger and Mike where it stood on its hind legs and roared as if insane. The thrown rider and some ring hands lunged and grabbed at the reins. Mike and Roger sat speechless. The horse was led away.

"What was that?" asked Mike, incredulously as they made their way to a beer garden on the second floor of the Horse Palace.

"A sign from God," answered Roger. "But I don't know of what."

They had three more beers and sat quietly at a little white table until the server cut them off and told them it was time to close down the oasis. Mike went in search of a washroom. Roger ducked under some ropes and went and sat against a wall in a vacant area where no one had bothered to set up a stall. Soon Mike joined him. Through a window open above them came the sound of thunder. Roger stood up and gazed out.

Fireworks were exploding against the night sky. Flashes of lightning illuminated the outlines of the bank towers downtown. The Midway lights were being shut down and a voice on the loudspeaker thanked everyone for making the year's Canadian National Exhibition a great success, and asking all to head to the exits. Throngs of ghosts crowded at the streetcar gates. Roger's heart sank. It was a vision of despair. His entire youth was ending within the hour.

"You know," he turned to Mike, speaking philosophically, "the summer is over. I wish I could make time stand still. I wish, that just for one moment, that tomorrow wasn't going to happen. We could go back to the ball park. We could sit there and wait and wait, and maybe linger an eternity, and the Jays would take it all. All of it. The whole fucking all of it."

Mike opened a sleepy eye. "Everyone thinks that."

"Yeah, but what if? Could you imagine it? All the suffering, all the patience, all the great dreaming and the great dreamers -- just one bloody perfect moment. That'd make time stand still. That'd be forever."

"Hey man," said Mike, "we are forever. This is forever." He let out a deep belch.

Roger looked back out the window. "No, not just that. Something else. Something more." He held out his hand to his friend and helped him up off the floor. They joined the columns of dark figures who made their ways home from the last night of the summer towards the labyrinths of mapled avenues where the leaves were dusty and full and rattled with prophecies of summers to come.

Roger did his Masters and went on to teacher's college before landing a job in Scarborough. Mike did well with the new firm in a bank tower at Bay and King. After a few years he was transferred as manager to a branch office in Saskatchewan. There were the usual Christmas cards. One might call the other on his birthday to wish him well. But the miles seemed so many, the distance greater with each passing year.

The wind was howling around the corner of Roger's apartment one night in the dead of winter. The telephone rang. Roger's wife answered. "It's for you," she said. "Some joker calling collect."

Roger took the receiver. "The charges from where? Okay, this had better be pretty good." His wife rolled her eyes.

"Did you hear?" asked a voice at the other end. "The Jays just signed Dave Winfield."

"Mike?"

"This guarantees them a shot at the whole thing. They'll be *there* in October."

They started to talk. There was so much to catch up on; Mike's first child, life in Regina, news of other friends.

"Do you really think they'll ever win?" asked Roger in despair. "They've been so close. Losing out to Boston, then Detroit. Being devasted by Canseco and the A's. So close and yet so far."

"Have faith. Hey, remember that old white horse at the Ex? You know, the one who went berserk and broke loose and pranced in front of us like it was trying to tell us something?"

"So?"

"I've figured it out. It was a sign from God."

"What did it mean? Have you been thumping a Bible out there or something?"

"No, no," retorted Mike. "It's like it was a portent. The way I see it, the horse was like everyone in Canada just busting to get loose. And it did."

"That's kind of pushing it a bit, isn't it? Wait a second there's some buzzing in my phone."

"What? I can't hear you."

Roger tapped the receiver of the phone. "There's some sort of interference on the line," he shouted into the mouthpiece. Distant voices as if filtered through static. They didn't seem to make sense. The wind whipped a white cloud by the window and snow beat against the pane like hoofbeats. "Can you hear it?"

"Yeah," said Mike, "but what's it all about? Listen..." And so they strained their ears to decipher the faint sounds that spoke as if coming from the deep past or far into the invisible future. "Listen..." And the sound grew just audible enough to hear.

Otis Nixon with the count two and two. The Braves down to their last bullet with this last chance to get something going. There's the pitch. Nixon the bunt! Timlin picks it up, tosses off to Carter at first. In time! For the first time, the championship flag will fly north of the border. The Jays win the World Series!

"Can you believe that?"

"I always believe," said Mike.

"Where did it come from?"

"From us, amigo. From us."

"Next year," said Roger as he put his free arm around his wife to give her a squeeze and realized that someday time would stand still, perfectly, beautifully still. "Next year will be glorious."

Father

The corner of Lehigh and Somerset has lost some of its old glory. Shibe Park, renamed Connie Mack Stadium in 1953, eighth wonder of the world to Philadelphians, has seen better days. There is a rumour that the American League A's will shift venue to Kansas City. On this day in August, the old team lies in last place and the humid summer of 1954 sits right on top of it. Cicadas sing their dirges in the trees and a wilderness of weeds multiplies in each vacant lot.

The old man in a grey suit and panama hat shuffles away from the gate and hails a cab. "Take me to St. Joseph's Academy, and go slow. I want to see what the old town's like now," he tells the driver in a gruff voice. Rows of houses file past, successions of porches and windows and front doors, an exhaustive monotony which makes the passenger shut his eyes. He dreams of the old days.

(His shadow was grey beneath the streetlamps as he stopped at a storefront window. It was a mistake to leave the Tigers. Philadelphia was fine, but it was too late. Zack Wheat was there. So was Tris Speaker and Eddie Collins. A gang from the glory days. A last hurrah. He had hit .323.

But the figure in the storefront window who stared back,1 was not the one who had once struck such fear, such awe in his opponents, had grown soft and round, a belly protruding and arms slackening. Only the fists were taut.

He had always seen himself the way the photographers did; a fire in his eyes as he slid into second with the dirt flying and the spikes high. Where was the man? Where was the demon? Had all the summers gone and left him with but this? The runs, the hits, the heckles from the crowd and terror in the eyes of his opponents. It had not been in vain. It had not been in vain...

And there, in the reflection, was not the image of the hero he saw, but that of his father, a stern, almost heroic figure in a three piece and watch-chain.

"*Do not come back a failure,*" *the father had warned the son. The warm southern night had been humid. His breath seemed to lie down and die with every word.* "*Do not come back a failure.*" *And now it had come to this.*)

The macadam ahead shimmers in the city heat and the traffic is snarled, so the cabbie swings onto a sidestreet only to discover that that passage is also barricaded by a game of stick ball and a gaggle of young boys. The driver rolls down his window as the taxi eases to a stop.

"You's kids dunno that they make diamonds for to play in and roads for to get killed in."

The boy in jeans and a striped shirt stands at an invisible plate and steps from the batter's box, wearing a look of annoyance. "In your face mister." He spits at the cab and a gob lands on the company name painted across the taxi's door.

"I'm coming back for you little shits. I'm warning you. Yous meat."

"What's it to you?" the old man hollers in a pronounced southern drawl from the back seat. "I ain't in a hurry. Let the goddamn kids play ball, yu'bastard."

The cabbie manuoevres around the gathering and the kids peer in. One of them raises a finger and the old man laughs to himself and mutters "Amen."

A tense silence fills the vehicle and the driver stares at his fare in the rearview mirror. The fare glares back. The old guy's eyes, thinks the driver, are like two dark coals burning a hole in the back of his neck. It is the cabbie whose nerves in this little game of silence and dislike fail first.

"You knows, its like I's seen you somewhere before? You gotta famous face or something?" The old guy turns and watches out the window. He hates idiots like this. He wants to be left alone. He wants to stare stonily at the world and defy what's left of time. He pulls his hat down over his face.

As the cab slows to the curb, the old man reads aloud the words "St. Joseph's Academy" etched in stone above a neo-gothic portal.

"Yeah," says the driver. "I'm sure of it. Yous the Peach, ain't you. Yeah. It's the goddamn Peach. 'My right? A real pleasure to meet you. Bet you still got it in you. I bet you do."

The old man snarls as he steps from the cab and tosses the fare through the front window. Dimes and quarters roll along the seat and spill to the floor. "Keep guessing, Mac, and let the kids play ball if they want." The passenger straightens up, hoists his pants northward over the protrusion in his torso and strides up the steps of the school. His back is straight, almost elegant, beneath the weight of the years.

"Hey! Hey!" the driver calls after the fare. The old man turns. For an instant, their eyes meet, and it is a look the cabbie will never forget, full of anger, passion, rage, disdain, mockery. The eyes say "Leave me be. I have a score to settle."

And beneath the terror that grips the driver's heart, he feels an instant of inexplicable elation. He is transported. He is no longer a middle-aged cab driver trapped in the labyrinthine streets of a city where his dreams were born only to die before their time, but a boy, hoisting a bat in a game of stick ball played beneath a scorching August sun. An instant before the pitch is thrown, he stares down the pitcher and shouts his threat: "Look at me, I'm Ty Cobb!"

The old man leaves the sunlight behind. He stands in the entrance way of the academy, its grey stone tomb-like and contrastingly cool after the humid light outside. He walks down the passageway as if he is stepping back in time; for that is his purpose here.

"You have an Al Travers around?" the old man demands of a secretary in the first room he comes to in the long hallway.

"A student?" she replies in a hushed, official tone as if this name were the secret of a lost identity.

"Pretty goddamned old if he was. I want to see him. I got some business with him, and its none of yours to ask what its about. Just bring me the sonnuvabitch. He's a preacher."

The secretary's face clouds. She pauses for a moment to think. "Oh, you mean Father Aloysius?"

The old man shrugs. "Whatever the hell his name is. I want to talk to him."

"Who should I say is here to see him?"

"Someone who assisted him in his ball playing days. You could say I made the guy's career," he adds, snickering to himself. The secretary does not get the joke.

She shows the visitor to a vacant office marked 'Dean' on the frosted glass panel of the door she closes behind her. The office is on the shady side of the building. The light, although bright, has a greyish-mauve, mournful cast. He seats himself in a chair which faces the desk and removes his hat, reaching into his pocket for a handkerchief to wipe away the beads of sweat. He examines the handkerchief and thinks to himself that he never sweated like this the last time he saw Al Travers.

(And the last time was May 18, 1912. The crowd was filing out of Shibe Park. The afternoon had grown overcast and the outcome had never been in doubt, not even before the first pitch. The pitcher paused for a moment and looked up into the stands and their eyes met. At that instant, it was as if they had shared some incredible understanding. The martyr and his temptor.

His team mates had gone back to the hotel to await their fate. After all, they'd walked out. They'd been the first players to go on strike in the American League. The baseball panjandrums did not take such stunts lightly. Perhaps, by the morning, they wouldn't have their jobs. But they had their team identity, and love him or hate him, they knew they couldn't play without their batting champion outfielder.

"Either Cobb plays or we don't," was the ultimatum they'd delivered a half hour before the game.

Jennings, the Detroit Manager, was distraught. He raced through the corridors of the park to find the office where American League President, Ban Johnson, was waiting for the game to begin. Something had to be done in a hurry.

Jennings was anxious to know what the price of forfeiture might be. Throngs of Philadelphia supporters and peanut vendors and lemonade hucksters barred his way as he fought a path to the owner's office. In full uniform, he removed his cap and knocked at the door.

Inside sat Ban Johnson, a powerful, rotund, chinless man propped like a god on a large chair. "Well?" he said and glared at the Tiger skipper.

Connie Mack, the gaunt, white-haired leader of the A's was there. He, too, was awaiting an answer. He wanted to know if the game points were his by default.

"They've walked. All of them," said Jennings with an air of defeat in his voice." Mack smiled.

The flush came into Johnson's cheeks. "Goddamit!" he screamed. "Jennings, you tell those sons of bitches you call a ball team that they either play today or they'll never play again, not in this league or the National. And, I'll underline it for them in black and white: no game today, no Tiger's franchise tomorrow."

Jennings scrunched his cap in his hands. "I've put my life into this club!"

"Yeah, but you can't put a team on the field."

"But what," and he realized he was grasping at straws, "what if I do field a team? What would you do then?"

Johnson considered for a moment. "Alright. You've got half an hour before game time. If you can find enough bums in that time, you can play. You won't lose the franchise. But I warn you, immediately after the game, you, me, Cobb and any other creep whose had a hand in this are going to meet and settle this issue once and for all. And that Cobb of yours who thinks he's bigger than the game has a rude awakening coming to him. To think he'd go after a fan like that and try to kill the guy. Shameful."

And for the entire game, Cobb sat in the stands ten rows up from first, cracking peanuts between the index and forefinger of his right hand, and watching as the crowd hissed and booed, then laughed at the debacle unfolding on the field.

But he saw something which he had been unable to forget since that eighteenth day of May in 1912. Half a lifetime ago.

The young pitcher leaving the mound at the end of a shattering day. A look on his face, not of defeat or humiliation or even exhaustion as Cobb might have expected, but of elation. Of joy. A light he had not seen since.)

Within moments the old man is restless, shifting from ham to ham on the hard wooden chair. He stares up at a crucifix on the wall where a dying Christ hangs in a moment of pitiable suffering. "What're you hanging around for," he says to the icon and chuckles sneeringly to himself.

He rises from his seat and walks to the window. He sees an older, slightly corpulent round-faced priest hurrying across the grass with the secretary not far behind. A gathering of ball players at the other end of a yard stand around the cage of a diamond as a batter takes practice and the outfielders shift to locate themselves beneath the flies. Within a minute, the door opens and the priest enters.

Breathless and smiling, the priest extends his hand to the visitor. "Good day, I'm Father Aloysius. You'll have to pardon me. I've been working on my outfield, and I think they're getting the knack of the angles."

"How old are they?"

"About sixteen, mostly, some seventeen year olds," says Father Aloysius as he seats himself in his official pose behind the desk and leans forward on the blotter, heaving huge breathless gasps between words. "Why do you ask?"

"If they don't know beans from shit at that age they never will. Can't teach an outfielder his skills. Has to come by it naturally. He either reads the ball or he doesn't."

"I see." The priest, whose lungs have caught up with him, folds his hands and adjusts his neck inside the startched white collar. There is a pause. The two men look at each other. "You are?"

"Here to see you," says the old man.

"Why?" asks the priest and blinks with raised eyebrows as if searching for the rest of the story.

"Can't say, really. I guess its about baseball. You've probably figured out who I am by now, but if you haven't, here's a clue. I'm the greatest goddamned baseball player who ever lived." There is a long pause. Both men smile.

"Mr. Cobb, it is a pleasure to meet you. What brings you to Philadelphia?"

"You."

"Me?"

"Yep." Both lean back in their chairs. "I was at your only game. So, it's Father Aloysius now, is it? Last time I saw you, you were nothing more than some stiff called Al Travers who happened to be wearing the finger of fate for an afternoon. You and me, well, I guess you could say that we're connected. We have a kind of destiny. You see, I was responsible for your ball playing career."

"I have to confess," said Travers, "I thought I recognized you. And, yes, I guess you could say that you were responsible." He chuckles. The visitor remains unhumoured. "That was a long, long day a long, long time ago." Another tense pause.

The sound of young voices on the diamond outside, mixed with the rumble of traffic and cicada song in the urban wilderness, punctuate the moment. The priest sees a lost moment in his mind. He tries to locate his age. He is almost twenty.

(He figured that he was early enough to see batting practice, perhaps pick up a few tricks or two that could be put to good use for his team. He was assistant manager for a seminary baseball club. On that day, Al Travers wasn't sure which road his life would take. He thought he'd make a good priest, but deep down he still wanted to be a ball player.

His steps quickened with excitement as he crossed the parkette at Lehigh and 21st. The flag was fluttering atop the ornate tower of Shibe Park, and the awnings were lowered against the bright May sunlight. He worked his way through the crowd that was settling itself in the stands, and took up a spot almost on top of the Tiger's dugout. There, he thought, he could hear the instructions being given to batters and pitchers. There, he would be able to eavesdrop on the professional genius of Detroit's manager, Hughie Jennings.

The Athletics, back to back World Champions, were already on the field. There was no sign of the Tigers. A frantic Jennings raced onto the field, carrying a megaphone cone in his hands.

"Are there any Tiger fans in the crowd? Are there any Tiger fans who would like a rare opportunity to see if they can make the team? Come down to the dugout right away." Travers stood up and waved and shouted and caught Jenning's eye.

"What position?" asked the Manager who took out a scorecard.

"I'm a pitcher," answered the young man. "I'm trying to hone my fastball into a weapon."

Jennings looked at him, and at the faces of the other young men who had gathered round to speak to him. "Boys," he said as he wiped his brow with his sleeve and replaced his cap, "we've got a little problem. The entire Tiger squad is indisposed today." There was a murmur among the assembled. "No, noth-

ing serious. Just that they aren't available to play. Who would like a shot at the majors? We'll pay you twenty dollars each for the game." Immediately, they all started shouting out their positions. "You, you, you and you, suit up." Jennings handed the batting order sheet to his base coach who took over the proceedings. "You," pointing to the eavesdropper, "you're my starter."

The Tiger dressing room was a silent place as the dozen nervous young men lifted the abandoned jerseys down from their hooks, right where the strikers had left them, and pulled them over their long johns. "So this is what a major league uniform feels like," he thought to himself. And silently they traipsed onto the field and the umpire shouted "Play ball!")

"You know," says Cobb with a sharp grin on his face and his eyes dancing, "you still hold the record for the most runs given up by a Detroit pitcher in a single game."

Travers rolls his eyes and laughs. "Yes, well, I try not to think about that. I try not to let Al Travers be confused with Father Aloysius."

"Why?"

"Why? Well, that was another time."

"You see, Father -- may I call you Father?" Travers nods. "You see, Father," Cobb continues, "although it really isn't part of my nature, or part of the nature I've made for myself which is how the world really sees me, I have to know. I've got a lot of questions. I'm coming to the end of my life. I've been told I have cancer. Cancer of this and cancer of that. I may not die of it immediately. Hell, I hope I don't die of it at all, and if I have anything to do with it I won't. But when the doctors told me, it started me thinking. It started me thinking about everyone I've known along the way, and what they'd make of me when it all added up. The baseball stuff is there in the record books for everyone to see and no one will ever touch that. No one. But there's all the other stuff. Part of me says forget about it, forget you're the biggest sonnuvabitch who ever walked the face of the earth. And then at night, when I'm all alone, and there's this silence, like everyone has gone home from the park and you're the last one standing there beneath the stars, that's when I start asking myself questions."

"What sort of questions, if I'm not prying by asking?"

"You know. The regular stuff. I tell myself, it's just the booze, its just the booze. But when the morning comes and I go for another blast of whatever's handy, those questions are still there. I feel pain inside me. I say no to the pain. But what about everyone else? By the way, I'm telling you this in confidence. If it ever came out that I cared about a single solitary human being other than myself, I'd be in the deepest shit of my life with everyone I've run over and railroaded and done the oskefagus on over the years." Cobb reaches into his breast pocket and pulls out a flask, uncorks it and swigs deeply. "Want some?" he says, holding it out to the priest.

"No thanks. So, why me?"

"You're safe and I just happened to be in town for an old-timers game. You are handy. And I've been thinking about that day of the strike. Sometimes at night, when I thought I was in hell and was trying to get used to the idea, I'd wake up and see you out there alone on the mound. You looked like him," says Cobb pointing to the crucifix. "Hung out to dry. I've never seen anyone so alone in my life. Shit almighty! They were blowing you out! Bam, bam, bam! I've never seen anyone so tortured in all my days. No sir. Bam. And I kept staring down at you, wondering when the hell is this stiff going to buck up and relinquish the field."

"It would have been easy to run away, especially after the first inning. But it was my moment and I had to live up to it. You know," says Travers, "they hit me around pretty hard that day. We had no fielding, not for that stuff, anyways. They were the Athletics. World Champs. Been very few clubs like that since. They sure knew how to place that ball. Where we weren't. I kept thinking every time they crossed the plate, 'Lord, let me find my fastball. Lord let me get it right just for once.'"

"So, you were praying!"

"Of course. Praying hard. I had only one pitch, a slider, and even that wasn't spotting well. I had been working on my fastball, but working on something and actually possessing it are two different things. Connie Mack was unmerciful. He just let them keep right on coming. His best line-up. I think he wanted to punish Detroit. I think he wanted to send a message to the world that only a professional can do a professional's job. But you're wrong to think I was alone out there. I was far from alone."

Goodbye Mr. Spalding

(*The A's had run the score up to 24. By some miracle, the Tiger side had bunted their way aboard in the fifth and landed a man on a walk, and Pennock, the A's pitcher, got rattled when they put on the double steal. Pennock only gave up two hits that day, the bunt and a single to centrefield. The centrefielder must have fallen asleep. Two runs came in to score. It was the high water mark in a slaughter.*

Connie Mack didn't complain when the inning ended. "You probably got tired waiting out there," he said and patted the fielder on the back. "I got tired waiting, too."

And when the Detroit at bat ended, Travers returned to his Golgotha. The mound rose up like a deathly hill beneath him. "Please, dear God," he prayed to himself, "give me my fastball. Give me the pitch I have sought so long. Just one moment. One moment of brilliance is all I ask. Allow me that. I will become a priest, but allow me to see what I might have been, just a glimpse, and I will give my life to you, gladly. I will be your servant."

At that instant, the pitcher sank to his knees and pressed his hands together, head bowed. The crowd rose to its feet. Was he breaking? Could he not stand the pain any longer? "The poor guy," someone said. Another yelled out "stop the insanity," and another: "this is a slaughter."

But Cobb was watching closely from his seat along the first base line. His eyes narrowed into tiny snake-like slits. They tensed and hardened. He could not understand. And the pitcher's lips were moving, whispering, and Cobb swore he could hear the words no one else in the stadium could understand: "Hail Mary, full of Grace," over and over.

Jennings started to walk onto the field. He turned and threw a daggerous look at Cobb in his perch along the first base line. Cobb sat steeley-eyed. "Are you alright, kid?" he asked, bending over his pitcher. "Have you pulled something?"

And as the word "Amen" issued from the pitcher's lips, he rose again and stood upon the mound, smiling, almost radiant, with a look of sublime confidence in his eyes. Jennings backed away, startled by what he saw. "Yes," Travers said to himself. "I know now what I will do."

On straight strikes he set the order down. The greatest order of the day. In the next inning, he shut them down again. And again in the eighth. For one brief, glorious moment, Al Travers found his fastball. "I know now," he said quietly to himself as he walked off the mound for the final time. "Thank you.

Thank you.")

"You may think it strange, Mr. Cobb, but you may be right. My secretary told me what you said. I may, in a way, have you to thank for all this. If you hadn't gone on strike I might have tried to make the bigs some other way. Sure, I'd given deep thought to the idea of becoming a priest. But something inside me kept saying, 'don't you want to know what it would be like to be a ball player, to have everyone cheering for you, to be a real somebody?' Huh, I used to think that being a ball player would make me a somebody. But there are so many other ways to that. So many other ways. I tell my boys when things don't go right, I tell them 'it's only a game. Your lives don't rest on this.' It's hard to convince a sixteen year old that the fate of the universe doesn't hang on his playing second base or having the hardest fastball. Who they are isn't just what they are on the field. But you know that."

Cobb swallowed hard. "So, Father, you weren't alone. How's that?"

Travers looks at his hands and smiles. "I guess you could say that I saw something. Like I said, I was trying to make up my mind. Priesthood or secular sainthood. I asked the Lord for help. I said to him, 'let me see, just for an instant, what it would be like to be, say, Ty Cobb?' It was great. I had good stuff. For only three innings, mind you. But it felt wonderful."

"So you struck a bargain with God, hey? God does deals after all," Cobb says eagerly leaning forward in his chair for an answer.

"No, Mr. Cobb, God doesn't do deals. In my case, I guess you could say he did me a favour. Call it grace. I consider what I experienced to be one of those rare waking visions, half absolution for a misplaced dream, half...whatever you want to call it. Providence, perhaps. There was my other dream, hanging there, tempting me in the heat. I could touch it, see it, smell it, taste it even. It was as if someone spoke to me and said 'this is not you,' no matter how good it felt. I heard 'this is not you.' And I realized that I didn't want to be anything other than what I am today. I found my peace of mind out there on the mound of Shibe Park. And I'm thankful for that everyday in my prayers."

"And besides," Travers continues, "even though I did find my fastball, the previous five innings had just about made up my mind that I'd be happier as a priest. I mean, twenty four runs is not the sort of thing one goes around bragging about. But I'm grateful, just the same, for having had a look-see at something else. It was like a vacation from myself. I got to be a hero for a few minutes, even if I was the only one cheering. That little bit of worldly vanity was just as much as... sorry. I didn't mean to imply that..."

"No, not at all. We're all vain sons of bitches out there on the field. We all want to be loved. You wanted to be loved. Depends on whose love you want. That's what I lived for, Father. And when I couldn't be loved, I really got a thrill out of being hated. Sliding into second and spiking some bastard in the groin and hearing him holler, 'I'm gunna kill you Cobb.' The devil in me loved it. And still, you know, the devil wants more. He's a hungry fuck. But, as my father always said, a man's not a man unless he sees all of himself. My devil's played my life for me. But I am also a man. And the man says 'look what you've done,' and the devil in me won't always let me see, but the man does. And it hurts. Father, it hurts. You know, just as you were talking now, for an instant I wanted to be you."

"Me?" asks Travers in surprise. "Whatever for?"

"You, Father, have the power of absolution. You can forgive. I've asked myself that a million times. 'Can you forgive those bastards?' Someone once said I would never be forgiven my wrongs until I learned to forgive others. Strange, eh? And every time the answer is no. It must be wonderful, what you have. That power. That power over yourself. You want to know why I came today? I wanted to meet you. I heard you'd become a priest. Priests don't talk out of school, do they? I want you to consider this a confessional. Father, will you hear my confession?"

"Anything you say, Mr. Cobb, I will hold in confidence."

"Good. That's good." Cobb pauses. He stares out the window. "I've had a battle. I guess you could call it a battle. Years and years now. A battle with myself. The devil and the man." Cobb paused. His shoulders heaved.

"Would it help if I asked you where your devil came from?"

"My father told me, Father, the last thing he said to me when I left to join the Tigers... Oh, he was all for me playing local ball. I guess he thought it would help his political career. 'Son of Local Leader Leading League.'That sort of thing. The last thing he said to me as I boarded the train north was 'Don't come back a failure.'"

"The pressure to succeed is always great."

"Hell, no! It wasn't that," roars Cobb on the verge of tears. He reaches into his pocket and searches for his handkerchief. His eyes are starting to cloud over. His eyes are full of Georgia moonlight.

(The man who emerges from the shadows of the southern night has forgotten his key. He fumbles in his waistcoat pocket and the fob of his great gold watch chain glints in the bluish shadows of the sweltering grapefruit moonlight. The door is locked, but he moves along the porch to the dining room window. The buffet is set with silver. There is stillness in the empty room. He rattles the window and finds it is unlocked. Slowly, slowly, he raises the sash. If he is quiet he will not wake his wife.

He removes his shoes and leaves them on the verandah. His coat sleeve brushes the porch swing and the chains sing like tiny warblers. He lays his hat on the swing so it will not be knocked off by the sash, and carefully, he puts one foot inside the house. And there in the light, he sees her. She is standing like a ghost in her long silk gown, the lace at her neck so delicate, so lovely. He says her name.

A sudden jolt and Cobb leaps up in bed. He is in a hotel room in Detroit, half the world away, he thinks. He is a success. His nightshirt is soaked with sweat and his nails have torn deep gashes in his chest. Father! he calls out, though no one hears him. Father! Father!

He reaches for the light. He has had a horrible nightmare. A woman is standing at the window, a smoking shotgun in her hands. She peers over the sill to see who she has shot. The silver petals of an old magnolia lie scattered on the porch, adrift in rivulets of bright red blood.)

"Father, Father," Cobb sobs out, clutching his hat brim into a crumpled bunch. "Father, I did not fail!"

Travers stands and moves around the desk. Cobb is seething and shaking. Tears are rolling down his cheeks. His entire frame heaves before he slips to the floor. Travers bends down and takes the visitor in his arms.

"Oh God in heaven," sobs the old man, "why did you do that to me? Why? Why?"

"There, there, it's alright. It's alright."

Cobb looks at the priest and tries to raise himself back into the chair. Travers pours a glass of water from a small jug and hands it to the crying man. "I'm sorry. I don't cry. I don't cry. It's just..." Cobb takes a deep breath. "The last thing my father said to me was 'don't come back a failure.' I was just a kid. I wanted, more than anything, to be loved by him. He was my hero. He was a titan of a man. But he never told me he loved me. I thought, maybe, just maybe if I go north and blow those bloody mother fuckers away, he'll see me for what I am. I didn't want to be a lawyer or a banker like he insisted. I wanted to play ball. I wanted to play and play and play and destroy any bloody fuckers who stood in my way. I wanted to show him. But my mother, my mother saw to it. In that awful belle silence of hers, she saw to it. She saw that I'd never be able to please him. Never be able to say 'there, you see? I am the greatest. I am a success. Now love me. Please love me.' But she killed him. She killed him on the day of my first game in the majors. Yes, you look shocked, but its true. She blew his heroic head all over the bloody magnolia bushes. They tried her. Tried her for murder. But I stood up. I stood there and defended her. I said they'd loved each other very much. But that was a lie. I think she was just looking for a reason to kill him. And that night he tried to break into his own home was just the excuse she needed. And that, Father, hey, listen to me calling you father. That, Mr. Al priestly Travers is when the devil took hold of me. That's when he took hold of my soul and my manhood and my skills and put them to his own use. And for just one minute, just one goddamned measly, fucking minute, I want to know what it would be like to say, 'I forgive you' to someone, to be able to spite the old demon in me. To feed the man inside who's hungered through the pain and the struggles and all the frenzy of my life, just to be able to stand up and say 'I forgive, I forgive,' and look myself in the mirror and know that the first absolution was for me. For me. For me."

Travers stands over Coob. "Forgiveness is there for the asking. Ask God for forgiveness. He'll give it. He will lift your weight."

"That's the problem. I don't trust the bastard. I've always figured that anyone who could allow such things to happen is not only dicing with human beings but fixing the cubes as well. I'd rather start with you and see how it feels." Cobb wipes his eyes and stares at the priest. "You first."

"For what?"

"For the way I caused you to be crucified that day on the mound at Shibe. You think it was just an accident that you were chosen that day. I hoped they'd find some sap to stand in there and try to fill the shoes of real ball players. And as you took the field, I thought to myself 'I hope this bugger really suffers.' And you did, at least for a while, and it made me feel great. It was the same feeling I'd had a few days before when I went into the stands in New York. There was this guy who kept hollering things. He accused my mother of having sex with a nigger. He shouted out that she killed my father to keep him quiet about the whole thing when he found out. That was as much as I could stand. My family, the family of Cobb's Legion and Georgia, we were all proud folk. We didn't field insults like they were squibbers at some practice. Life was war to us all. And I grabbed a bat and went after the little shit. And I beat on him and beat on him and all the time he was hollerin' for mercy. Then somebody pulled me away. The guy didn't have any hands. Ha! Look Ma! No hands! It's always cowards who shout the loudest when it comes to defaming a person's character. That little bugger had a mouth on him, but no hands."

"What happened then?"

"They suspended me. Ban Johnson, the high and mighty President of the American League. And Hughie Jennings went along with the whole deal. 'Cobb, you're out.' Just like that, as if I didn't matter to the game. But my team mates knew they couldn't win without me. I gave them character. I put the fear into the other teams. So they stood by me. And they walked out."

"They struck in support of you."

"You're damn right. Not because they loved me, but because they were afraid I'd kill them with a gun I still keep with me." Cobb opens his jacket pocket and shows Travers the pistol. "Luger. I once pistol-whipped a man to death in Detroit when he tried to rob me." Travers draws in a breath in shock. "Anyways," Cobb continues, "they walked. They couldn't ban me from the park. So I sat and watched.

I watched you, because your suffering gave me glee. Only, toward the end, that God of yours had different ideas. He took your pain away from you and gave it to me. The humiliation. The belittlement. And now I covet what you got that day. I want your calm. Deep. In here," he pounds at his chest. "I want to be forgiven."

"But the League took you back."

"Of course they took me back. I was bigger than the game. I still am. It takes an unforgiving sonnuvabitch to make a statement like that. Only..."

"Only you're not one. Are you, Mr. Cobb. I believe there is a man inside you. You may not believe in God, and heaven forbid you should even find it in you to love Him. You are going to have a lot of accounting to do for yourself before you will be able to come around to Him. I can help you. I will pray for you."

"And will you forgive me? Forgive me, Father, for I'm such a bastard. Forgive me for tempting you like a snake in the tree of life or a demon in the desert of your worst moment by holding out to you the eternal possibility of what you could have been in spite of yourself. Ha! I think you are too damned proud to look me in the eye and accept the apology of your temptor. I, the one whose actions directly or indirectly led you to your God when what I really wanted was for you to walk away and curse the Almighty, so I could say that I'd won a real victory that day. A real win. And I didn't even have to put on my cleats. C'mon, I dare you. Forgive me."

"Mr. Cobb," says Travers in a calm, reassured voice, "you may have set the events in motion which held out the vision of temptation to me, but it was a vision I could deny. Both the man and the priest in me are strong enough." Travers moves toward Cobb who holds out his hand as if to accept a shake. But Travers does not take Cobb's hand. Instead, he places his right palm on the southerner's forehead. "In the name of the Father and of the Son and of the Holy Spirit," and smiles benevolently at the visitor. "If it is forgiveness you seek, I offer it to you. If it is absolution you desire, perhaps I can help you find it. I hope you will find the peace of mind you crave so much. Seek it through God."

Cobb sits still for a moment, staring straight ahead of him. He has a distant look in his eyes. "God's a long, long way away. You, at least, are closer. The man in me is grateful." Together they are silent for a time.

"Would you like to see the team," asks Travers as he shrugs one shoulder toward the open window. "I have an outfielder who could be quite fine, if only for a little advice."

And Cobb speaks. His voice is remote, calm, lacking in the cantankerousness that underscored his earlier talk. "I'd like that," he says. They rise together and leave through the door.

As they cross the yard to the diamond, Cobb turns to his host and asks, "You still enjoy the game?"

"Very much, Mr. Cobb. Very much. It is one of the great joys in my life."

"And what, pray-tell, is the purpose of joy for you?"

"The purpose of joy is to find life, and the purpose of life is to discover joy. That's where baseball comes in. That's God's place too. Think of it this way. You have a beautiful summer day. Everything is perfect for a game. The stands are full. The sun is shining. The batter gets a piece of an inside curve, and the ball takes off. It rises and rises, but everyone watching just knows it's going foul. There's the foul pole. There's the ball. But suddenly, out of nowhere, even though the flags are limp and you could swear there isn't a breath moving in the place, something catches that foul ball and pulls it fair. And you just know a miracle has happened. That's joy, Mr. Cobb. Pure, inexplicable joy."

And as they near the diamond, one of the boys drops his bat and points. "There's Ty Cobb. Father Aloysius has Ty Cobb with him!" Suddenly they are mobbed.

"You see," says Cobb grinning like a jackal to the priest, "they still love me. They always will."

(There is no park now at Lehigh and Somerset where Al Travers pitched his only major league game and where Ty Cobb, exhausted and broken from fighting his demons too hard for too long played out the final chapters of his illustrious career for Connie Mack's Athletics.

In the vacant lot, a city block square, the weeds have grown thick and brown, risen and died, and risen again and spread their seeds through countless summers of fathers and sons and baseball games. A few curious nostalgia seekers appear each year to pace off the confines of the lot, to recall famous plays and recollect lost times.

Whatever they are seeking is only a vision now. Often, they remark that in the centre of that weedy patch is a rise in the level ground. Some say this is the old mound of Shibe Park. And there, the grass will not grow upon its pale, bald skull.

But where the scoreboard used to count the numbers for and against the homeside heroes, a group of optimistic evangelists have erected a tiny chapel to call the Lord's name in that wilderness where Paradise once stood. And they name that place 'Deliverance.')

About the Artist

Arthur Burdett Frost (cover and frontice piece) was born in Philadelphia, January 17, 1851 and began his career as an artist by illustrating books. He studied part-time at the Pennsylvania Academy of Fine Art and in London in 1877, but was primarily self-taught. He received an honourable mention at the Paris Exposition of 1909. His works include illustrations for *Uncle Remus, Tom Sawyer* and *Mr. Dooley.* He died in Passadena, California on June 22, 1928. For the cover painting, "The Critical Moment," (1907), Frost wrote an accompanying verse:

> Herbert Johnson, Herbert Johnson
> You've got a glorious deed to do—
> If you miss it—if you miss it—
> Local pride is watching you!
> Gosh, you've caught it! Gee you've
> tagged him!
> Herbert you're a hero now.
> Hip, hooray for Herbert Johnson
> And the Cornville Eagles—WOW!

About the Author

Bruce Meyer is author of ten books including the poetry collections *The Open Room* (1988) and *Radio Silence* (1992) and co-author with Brian O'Riordan of the interview collections *In Their Words* (1985) and *Lives and Works* (1992). He teaches English in the University of Toronto at Trinity College, and is an instructor at Seneca College and the School of Continuing Studies. He lives in Toronto with his wife, journalist Kerry Johnston.